PANDORA'S BOX

SCOTT R. HOWE

Copyright © 2022 by Scott R. Howe

All rights reserved. No part of this publication may be reproduced, stored or transmitted in any form or by any means, electronic, mechanical, photocopying, recording, scanning, or otherwise without written permission from the publisher. It is illegal to copy this book, post it to a website, or distribute it by any other means without permission.

This novel is entirely a work of fiction. The names, characters and incidents portrayed in it are the work of the author's imagination. Any resemblance to actual persons, living or dead, events or localities is entirely coincidental.

First edition

ISBN: 9798759876014

Editing by James Merk
Additional editing by Susan Howe
and Rebecca Goodchild
Story Consultants: Angela Ortner
and Rebecca Goodchild

Cover Design: Scott R. Howe

This novel is dedicated to my parents; my mother, Joanne, who loved books and encouraged me to write my own one day, and my father, Robert, who instilled in me a love of scary movies.

This novel is also dedicated to survivors of sexual assault, both known and unknown.

www.RAINN.org
800-656-HOPE

"One need not be a chamber to be haunted."

— Emily Dickinson

Contents

Acknowledgement		iii
1	The Body	1
2	7 North Goodman Street	3
3	Unpacking	12
4	The locket	22
5	Revelations and More Questions	32
6	Mary, Mary Quite Contrary	37
7	Sanctuary	40
8	The housewarming	48
9	Light and shadow	59
10	The Realization	67
11	The Boogeyman	71
12	And Pretty Maids All in a Row	81
13	A Secret	83
14	With Silver Bells and Cockleshells	85
15	Louise	87
16	Alex	97
17	Chloe	113
18	Sleepover	120
19	Pandora's Box	133
20	Digging a Hole	141
21	Despair	143
22	Nightmares	152
23	Revelations	159

24	The Scene of the Crime	164
25	Digging deeper	169
26	A Way Forward	175
27	Pandora's Box	187
28	Hunting the Scarecrow Killer	199
29	The Scarecrow	211
30	A new beginning	216
31	Epilogue	219
Bibliography		221

Acknowledgement

I've always wanted to write a book but felt it was too presumptuous to try. I'd never considered myself a writer. My mom was one of my biggest supporters while I was growing up; she made me believe that I could do anything I set my mind to, but writing a book still seemed out of reach. Ever since I can remember, I've always enjoyed Halloween, the paranormal, and horror. My dad instilled in me a love of movies, starting with King Kong, which sparked an interest in film history and, by my early twenties, a near obsession with the silent film actress, Louise Brooks. Finally, it dawned on me that I could combine all of my greatest interests: a fascination with Louise Brooks and with film history, my long-held belief in the paranormal, and a love of horror in general. After that, everything else came very fast, and I had completed a first draft in a matter of months. Getting it to the point where it could be published, however, required a lot of support from family and friends along the way.

I owe a huge debt of gratitude to those who provided me with detailed and constructive feedback throughout the writing process. Jim Merk read through my original manuscript twice, as he likes to remind me, and he gave me a lot to think about – and to work on. From there, the book went to my sister, Susan Howe, who made sure this book was finished without me sounding like a complete idiot, and who was instrumental in helping me with rewrites and consistency; my sister-in-law, Rebecca Goodchild, worked tirelessly with me on rewrites, tweaks and ultimately made sure I got the most out of every creepy moment; and Angela Ortner, who helped me through my first draft, proved, once again, why she makes the perfect creative story partner.

I'm also thankful to my sister-in-law, Judy Howe, and my friends, Brian Tomono, Sanjeev Kriplani, Michelle Luzania Maksymowicz, Laura Landon and Suzanne Adan, who each read through various stages of my original drafts and encouraged me to keep going and provided me with valuable comments and support along the way.

I'd like to acknowledge my grandmother, Hazel French, who inspired the character Hazel in my novel; and my brother, Steven Howe, who, for years, has taken great joy in goading me that nobody, other than me, really knows who Louise Brooks is — his constant teasing refrain: "Louise Brooks – the actress that time forgot."

I'd also like to thank my friends Brad Clark, Larry Hicks, Kelsey Lindelof and Damien Espinoza, each of whom offered me wonderful subject matter insights and, in some instances, unintended character inspiration.

Finally, I want to thank my wife, RuiXia, for supporting me and keeping me alive throughout COVID-19; and my daughter, Dr. Jodi Mao, M.D., for constantly providing me an incentive to strive for excellence.

In terms of my 30-plus year fixation with Louise Brooks, this book has done a lot to scratch an itch. Time will tell whether it was merely scratching the surface.

1

The Body

The body in Apartment 307 was discovered by a neighbor across the hall. It was the early hours of Thursday morning — August 8th, 1985. The remains belonged to an elderly woman who had been a virtual recluse for most of the last thirty years. She'd left her apartment so infrequently, in fact, that few people could even describe her or recollect her name. Only the neighbor who had discovered her had taken a personal responsibility during the last few years to check in on her each night to make sure she'd eaten and to aid her each morning, making sure she'd had enough to eat for breakfast.

The woman died in her sleep of natural causes hours before, but her gaunt, tortured appearance suggested otherwise. Her mouth gaped open, as if she'd spent her last moments gulping for air. Her arms were crossed over her chest, and her right hand was clenched into a twisted, bony fist.

A half-full glass of water, two unopened prescription

medicine bottles, a notepad, and a pen were on the bedside table. Two aluminum walking canes leaned against the wall near a small closet.

Except for a small, framed reproduction of a Man Ray painting that hung opposite the bed, the walls were bare, and the dominant color in all three rooms of this austere, 850-square-foot apartment — the walls, the ceiling, and the furniture — was a dull pink. A somewhat frayed pink night coat was spread on the bed close to the woman's body.

Aside from the neighbor who had found her, nobody living at the building on North Goodman Street knew who the woman was, much less that she'd been a Ziegfeld Follies dancer, a silent film femme fatale, and later a writer, or that she'd had an affair with Charlie Chaplin when he was at the height of his career — and she was just nineteen.

2

7 North Goodman Street

Emily was pressed for time. She'd recently resigned from her job and taken a new one, ended a two-year relationship with Alex, and relocated five and a half hours away, in Rochester, New York. She wasn't looking for an extravagant place to live. For now, modest would suffice. Her withdrawal from New York City had been hurried, and under such circumstances, she could not afford to be too particular. Emily had already spent a month in Rochester with her former graduate school roommate, Chloe, and she was beginning to fear that she would soon outstay her welcome. She and Chloe were now coworkers at the same news media outlet, and she didn't want to be a burden to her best friend, who had always been her go-to shoulder. She'd spotted an apartment online that looked to be reasonably priced, and it was located only ten minutes from her new workplace.

From her car, she peered up at the unassuming, dingy white

brick building at 7 North Goodman Street and thought to herself with slight amusement that she and the building would make a good pair.

She wore her shoulder-length auburn hair straight with it parted on the side and the rest tucked behind one ear. She generally preferred to dress for comfort. Some of her friends, however, would have described her look more as sixties-not-so-chic. On this day, as on most days, she'd decided not to wear lipstick. When she was a child, people, even strangers, had told her that she was beautiful. The attention made her want to keep to herself and led her to dress for comfort rather than style and to avoid wearing makeup, a preference that lasted into adulthood.

Since she was on her own and would be driving more often now, Emily bought a car soon after arriving in Rochester. The car, a used yellow Volkswagen Bug, was a great fit for her — just the right size for her slight build.

Emily took a look around and liked the appearance of the street. She hoped she would like the apartment as much as the look of the neighborhood. The apartment manager was scheduled to see her at 1:30, but he had called to tell her that he was running late. Emily chose to take a stroll around the outside of the apartment complex while she was waiting.

Although it wasn't immediately apparent from the ground, she knew from an aerial photo she had seen when she first looked up the address on her phone that the footprint of the complex resembled a plus sign. The building had six stories aboveground. She could see that there was a metal garage door entrance along the other side that led under the building. Online, Emily read that there were communal washers and dryers. She speculated that they were located in the basement garage.

From the front, tucked into an inside corner, a small set of cement stairs led up to a concrete landing, where she could see there was a commercial storefront-type glass entrance. Above the entry was a sturdy cement slab awning painted in turquoise — the only thing giving the building any color at all.

Emily liked that there were a few tall trees in front of the building that could provide some much-needed shade throughout the day and soften the harsh, almost industrial feel of the building. When she looked up, something in one of the windows caught her attention. Emily could see someone gazing down at her from the third floor. As their gazes locked, the tall form drew slightly back behind one of the partially opened curtains. The figure, who appeared to have the build of a man, but who was still mostly hidden in shadow, had not, however, ceased looking down at Emily, and she began to feel uneasy. She raised her hand to wave, but before she could observe the form's reaction, she heard a voice calling her name.

"Emily Pierson?"

Emily snapped her attention toward the voice to see an older, bearded, bespectacled gentleman dressed in a sweater vest and tie.

"Are you Emily? I'm Richard. We chatted on the phone. Sorry again about the delay."

Emily smiled, as if to emphasize that she had not been inconvenienced. She thought he looked rather proper, not at all what she expected him to look like from their brief conversation on the phone. She half-expected him to speak with an English accent.

She cocked her head and once more glanced up the third-floor window. The figure was gone. Then she walked toward the landlord, her hand extended.

"I see you're already getting familiar with the apartment for rent," he said as they shook hands.

"Sorry?" she said.

"The apartment I have available is number 307, the windows at the front corner there, where you were just looking."

"But I saw someone up there in that window just now. Does the current tenant still live there?" Emily asked.

"No," the landlord said, shaking his head. "Besides," he continued with a small grin, "you're the only one on my calendar for today, so there shouldn't be anyone in that apartment."

Emily considered whether her imagination was deceiving her, or if the sun's reflection on the glass had simply given her the mistaken sense that someone was up there. She knew, for instance, after fact-checking for a recent story, that pareidolia, a human need to see recognizable patterns and familiar shapes in clouds and other such things, was frequently cited as a reason for such misidentifications. Her mind must have been playing tricks on her.

The landlord strolled beside Emily as they made their way back around to the front entrance. He motioned for her to climb the small set of concrete stairs and then thumbed through his set of keys for the master that would open the double-paned glass doors in front of them.

"If you become a tenant here, you'll receive a key similar to this one to gain access to the building. This key also works for the back entry in the basement garage."

He directed his attention to the button panel next to the glass door and continued, "If you have visitors, they can punch in your apartment number on the intercom system. The buzzer will sound in your apartment; you can press the button just inside the door to unlock the entrance to the lobby, and they can find their way up."

Emily's eyes adjusted to being inside, and she could now see the lobby. She scanned the room. Green wall-to-wall broadloom sculptured carpeting with a floral design covered the floor, suggesting a bygone era. Emily's gaze was then pulled to the beautiful old elevator doors. They were decorated with etched art deco designs in brass.

As she looked around, she thought to herself that the lobby reminded her of the apartment lobbies she'd seen in 1940s films: sparse, but with an air of upscale luxury, as if the room were attempting to convince anyone entering that they'd entered a building with more distinction than it actually possessed.

As they stepped into the elevator, Emily jumped when the iron-cage doors clanged shut behind her. As they rode the elevator to the third floor, she struggled to focus on the landlord's descriptions of rose bushes that surrounded the property and how they were planted there when the building was first opened to tenants. She was too distracted by the way the elevator's light kept flickering as if it would short out any moment. The elevator's lighting was weak, lending an air of dinginess to the tight, confined space. Emily watched as the numbers crept from one to two and then to three. As the doors opened onto the third floor, she felt relief that the ride was over. The landlord indicated that "her" apartment was just down the hall and to the right.

Emily waited in front of the door to apartment 307, watching the landlord fumble to locate the correct key. After a few moments, he said, "Here we go," unlocked and opened the door, and waved Emily inside.

As she entered, she glanced swiftly about the empty space. Her initial reaction was that it was a little smaller than she had anticipated. Within this little common area, one wall served as the basis for a kitchen, with a modest refrigerator, a sink, and a narrow cabinet above the sink and countertop. In addition to all of that, there was a tiny electric stove and oven combination. Walking down the corridor to her right, she noticed a small bathroom with a shower/tub combination. To the left of that was a bedroom with an adjacent closet, barely big enough to accommodate the contents of a suitcase. Emily noted that each room had windows that brought much-needed light — and vitality — into this space. She walked into the bedroom to the window and looked down at her car. It seemed to be the same window and draping she had seen from the outside when she noticed the man watching her. She glanced down at the windowsill, and in the thin layer of dust, she noticed a faint smudge that resembled a fine handprint. Curious, she placed her hand alongside the print and noticed it was the same size as her own. Emily resolved that when she got back down to the street, she would check the third-story windows one more time, to see if the figure she had seen previously was actually in this apartment.

She returned to the main area as the landlord described the different features of the apartment. He listed the refrigerator, sink, and stove, and Emily nodded, primarily out of politeness. After the initial shock of discovering how much smaller the space was in comparison to the images she had seen online, Emily began to consider the possibilities of the space. Though it first appeared to be too tiny for the furniture she'd envisioned, suddenly the apartment appeared to be more adorable. As long as she avoided crowding the area with too much stuff, she thought, this space might accommodate her very well.

Leaning against the wall, the landlord locked his attention on Emily. "So, Miss Pierson," he said. "Are you new to Rochester?"

Still gazing around the room, Emily answered with a smile, "I am."

"So, you didn't grow up around here?"

"I grew up in Kansas."

"Kansas," repeated the landlord. "So, this must be quite different from what you're used to." Then he added with a chuckle, "There's no place like home…."

"I'm sorry?" said Emily, only half paying attention.

"Oh, well… just, you know… Kansas…? *The Wizard of Oz*…?"

Emily responded with the appropriate polite laugh; she'd become accustomed to hearing allusions to *The Wizard of Oz* over the course of a lifetime of disclosing her Kansas roots. Emily, on the other hand, preferred the Emerald City to Dorothy's desire to go home.

"I guess I sort of skipped a bit in between…" said Emily in a self-effacing tone.

"I didn't exactly arrive here straight off a bus from Wichita or anything," Emily said, adding, "I've been working in Manhattan for the last few years."

"Oh… I see," said the landlord. "So, you're no stranger to city life."

"That's right."

After a slight pause in the conversation, the landlord began again. "Are you here for work?"

Emily nodded.

"What sort of work do you do?" The landlord paused for half a beat, then continued, "If you don't mind my asking."

"Not at all. I usually just tell people I'm a fact-checker. It's easier than trying to explain."

The landlord's blank expression told Emily that she should probably explain further, but she instead returned her attention to investigating the apartment. She continued, "I know it's not the most glamorous job in the world, but it's solitary work, which suits me."

"I would've pegged all of you millennials as more of the 'out front' sort," the landlord said.

"'Out front'?" Emily asked.

"You're much too young to be hiding in the shadows, don't you think?" said the landlord.

"I prefer to keep to myself," she replied. Then she added, smiling, "My past landlords have appreciated that."

He paused for a moment. "Constantly checking facts, as you do, well, you must be a walking encyclopedia," he said.

"Not really. But I'm pretty good at looking things up." Then she added with a laugh, "No, I guess you're right. I do probably have a lot more useless information in my head than the average person."

The landlord brightened. "Did you know that Susan B. Anthony is buried in our Holy Sepulchre Cemetery, not far from here?"

"Actually," said Emily, "*she's* buried in Mount Hope Cemetery, but you know who *is* buried at Holy Sepulchre? Francis Tumblety!"

The landlord looked confused. "I'm sorry, who?"

With a hint of mystery in her tone, Emily answered, "He's long been regarded a major suspect in the Jack the Ripper murders."

The room fell silent as the two exchanged uncomfortable glances.

Emily laughed again. "This is why I'm rarely invited to parties."

The landlord spoke with a bit of a chuckle. "Miss Pierson, I believe you would be an excellent addition to the building."

Emily took a deep breath and inspected the apartment one final time before signing the rental contract which the landlord had brought with him. She felt confident it would be a comfortable home for her. She smiled as the landlord closed the front door behind them, and handed her the keys to number 307. This, she decided, represents the start of something new.

In her rush to return to the other tasks on her to-do list, Emily climbed back into her car and failed to take another glance at the bank of windows on the third floor.

If she had remembered to inspect the windows on her way out, she would have seen the same figure observing her departure from the bedroom she had stood inside just minutes earlier. As Emily drove away, the curtain in the window closed.

3

Unpacking

"Trick or treat!" they yelled as Emily opened her door. This latest group of miniature superheroes, witches, and fairytale princesses couldn't tell through the little eye holes in each of their masks that the bowl Emily held just above their greedy gaze was nearly empty. She looked down, for a moment, to take them all in. A miniature cowboy had some of his leather fringe caught on his sister's fairy wand, which made Emily smile.

Emily quickly counted heads. *Shit*, she thought to herself; she had grossly underestimated the number of children who would be living in this apartment building. It was her first week in the new place, and she knew it wouldn't go well if word got out that the new girl in apartment 307 had cheated some couple's poor child out of his or her due treat.

"Look how scary you all are," she said, pausing just long enough to count the pieces of candy in her bowl. Perfect, she realized; there was just enough candy left to give each child two pieces. Emily received a polite, if mostly muffled, "thank you" with each thud of candy into outstretched plastic Jack-O-Lanterns. The last child took his treat, turned around, and marched down the hall to the next apartment door, trailing behind the rest of them.

Emily smiled as she watched the last of them round the corner, and then she shut her door. "The candy store is closed," she said to herself. It was nearly nine o'clock, long after most children would have gone trick-or-treating. She figured that if any more children came knocking, she would simply not answer the door. No one would think less of her if she didn't answer the door after nine o'clock. For all anyone knew, the new girl in apartment 307 was probably out having her own good time, celebrating Halloween the normal way…getting shit-faced and passing out on a random friend's couch.

That wasn't really Emily's style. And with her recent break from Alex too fresh to allow her to consider celebrating much, a quiet evening at home seemed like the ideal way to spend the rest of the night. After all, there was still a little more unpacking to do.

She went to the kitchen to get a beer from the fridge. As she closed the refrigerator door, she glanced at the box labeled "STUFF" that was sitting atop the kitchen table. She broke apart the masking tape and peered inside. There were the expected tchotchkes and stray items, but there was also a picture of her and Alex that she'd forgotten she'd thrown into this box. The happy couple in the photo smiling back at her seemed almost unrecognizable to her now. Alex's sandy hair was still mussed up even though she'd tried to fix it. She could remember laughing at him as she ordered him to bend a little so she could reach the top of his head. He never worried about such things, though. He always managed to look handsome in Emily's eyes, no matter what. She hadn't smiled like she had in that picture in a long time, and now, she couldn't even imagine being touched by Alex. She remembered hastily grabbing things from the refrigerator door at the old apartment — the apartment they both shared until just a month ago. Her memories of that day flooded back to her.

She knew Alex's work schedule at Hutchins, Needam and Mao; he wouldn't return for several hours, and it was the one day that week she'd be off from work and would have the apartment to herself. That would be her opportunity to gather her things, as only then could she do so without his knowing. If all went according to plan, she'd be halfway to Rochester before he returned home to discover she'd gone.

Emily had felt distant from Alex for some time before she made the decision to leave him. Something had gone wrong, but she wasn't yet sure what. When they met in graduate school and began dating, Alex possessed all the characteristics she'd hoped for in a partner. He was kind, well-educated, and focused on establishing a career. She'd always found Alex handsome, and the fact that he was so attentive was thrilling. While unaccustomed to receiving wanted attention from guys, she found her biggest cheerleader in Alex. In many respects, he was essential in reestablishing her confidence since men had not offered her the type of devotion she'd always believed was reserved for others, and not her.

On the five-and-a-half-hour drive to Rochester, she thought about her past. Emily was a bit of an odd bird in middle school. She was quiet and withdrawn, often preferring to be alone. This pattern continued through high school, even continuing on through college and graduate school, well after she'd left Cherryvale, Kansas.

She hadn't always been this way; when she was young, she was a gregarious child — and very active. She'd always been precocious, and while her parents had become accustomed to all the odd questions from their overachiever, even *they* couldn't answer them all. Her mother quipped that if it hadn't been for their close friendship with their next-door neighbors, the Harrises, Emily would have been too much for any two parents to handle on their own. Emily spent a lot of her spare time at the Harrises'. They didn't have any children of their own, and Bonnie Harris relished her role as Emily's surrogate aunt. They would even spend time, sometimes well into the evening, gazing at stars from the Harrises' front porch, and Emily could be heard giggling and carrying on, asking about every constellation she could find.

By the time she had turned twelve, however, Emily's disposition had shifted, and this trend continued through middle school. She developed an introverted and quiet demeanor and withdrew into her books. Her teachers assured her parents that such behavior was typical of intelligent teens who might not be into the usual social activities of middle school. Although her parents still felt something was off with their daughter, they agreed to defer to the advice of the teachers.

Emily was an outsider by the time she reached high school. She was attractive, but she never did anything to enhance her appearance, and she was so withdrawn that no one knew how to approach her. Emily's aura had become like a second skin to her, and she was relieved that it helped her stay invisible.

Emily longed to flee and to reinvent herself in a new place. She sought a type of renaissance. Though she'd always reveled in the role of the obedient daughter, she longed to be someone who was carefree and independent instead of someone who felt trapped by the persona she'd fallen into. She was an exceptional student throughout high school and was granted a full scholarship at Wichita State. There, she imagined, she would finally be able to escape her self-imposed exile and recreate herself in a fresh environment, away from people who had long since cast her off as a quiet loner. Her parents were ecstatic that she would be attending college close to home. Emily initially felt the same way. However, she acquired an appetite for something more along the way. Something that Kansas was incapable of providing. After graduating from Wichita State, she wanted to continue her education, but this time she made sure it would be far from home. She was admitted to the University of Wisconsin-Madison and left Cherryvale immediately.

Emily flourished in her new environment and discovered her calling: journalism. She enjoyed investigating stories, vetting people, and generally being able to live in a world of facts. It was in graduate school that she met Alex, and they became serious rather quickly. This was completely uncharacteristic of her. Whereas before, she stuck to her room, or spent all her time in her favorite carrel in the library, after she met Alex, she relished spending time on the quad, making up crazy dance moves in an effort to make Alex and her roommate, Chloe, laugh.

Chloe liked Alex, but she still felt the need to warn Emily about getting too serious, too fast. Chloe remarked to her that "when first struck, a match burns brightly, but tends to flame out quickly." Emily wasn't having any of it. She was in love, and they were going to plan a life together. After graduate school, they all left for New York state; Chloe went to Rochester to pursue an on-camera reporter position at WROC TV Channel 8, and Emily and Alex found their home in the trendy Manhattan art district of Chelsea, in the heart of New York City. Emily worked as a fact checker, deep inside the bowls of 30 Rockefeller Plaza where she worked behind the scenes of one of the MSNBC morning mid-day programs, and Alex landed an internship with a law firm and later was hired as a full-time associate, upon passing the bar. And for more than a year, the flame that had characterized Emily and Alex's relationship in the beginning was still going strong.

At first, everything felt perfect, but the intensity of their new jobs kept them apart frequently, and Emily began to feel as if they were just going through the motions of being a couple. Alex seemed more like a roommate than a romantic partner. He'd been spending an increasing amount of time "at work" or "with his friends," and Emily felt virtually alone in the months leading up to her leaving. She'd become a ghost in a romance that had most likely ended before she realized what had happened and just hadn't pieced together the evidence yet.

In the weeks preceding her leaving, Emily alternated between feeling virtually alone to feeling nervous and anxious whenever Alex was home. She suspected that he was cheating on her. And when she found a receipt to her favorite restaurant in his pants pocket, dated the same night she was working late on deadline, Emily determined that she'd not sit idly by while her man was with another woman. She wasn't going to wait for things to get worse and then make accusations that he would surely deny.

She wasn't going to be made a fool, so she resolved to get

out before this hollow relationship had time to fully implode — and she'd do so quickly, while he was at work, so she could disappear and avoid all conflict when he arrived home and saw that she'd gone.

Her thoughts returned to the refrigerator door in her old apartment, where she had originally taped the photo. On the day that she moved out, she hastily threw the last of her things into random open boxes with little concern over what to do with any of it; she'd sort it all out later. She'd stuffed the photo into this last box, along with the last few belongings that had suddenly become hers, and no longer theirs.

Three loud knocks on the front door shattered the silence and vibrated through the kitchen walls. "Shit!" she exclaimed, startled. Her beer almost slipped from her grasp. That couldn't be a trick-or-treater, she thought, not this late in the evening. She took a look at her phone. It was nearly ten o'clock. She wondered if she had really been standing in the kitchen for an hour.

BANG, BANG, BANG!

Emily remained motionless for a brief moment. Suddenly, panic washed over her, and she wondered if she'd done something to disturb one of the neighbors. But then she had a thought: What if Alex had found her? She moved over to the door and carefully peered through the peephole, trying not to make any noise that would alert the person on the other side that anyone was home. Looking down, she saw a young girl. Her panic drained away quickly.

"You've got to be kidding," she murmured to herself. Emily grew irritated that someone would let such a small child out to go trick-or-treating at such a late hour, but she was glad that it was just that — and not who she'd feared was on the other side of the door. Despite the fact that Emily had depleted her candy supply, her curiosity was getting the better of her, and she desired a closer look at the small child standing at her door. This one seemed different from the others she'd already seen this night. She reached up to unlock the door, still gazing through the peephole.

"Just a sec, sweetie," she said.

As the door swung open, Emily tried to think of the best way to tell this pretty little child that the free handouts were over.

"I'm sorry, honey," she said with a sad, soft tone. "I have no more candy."

She crouched to bring her eyes down to the small child's level. The girl was probably seven or eight years old. When she examined this child's outfit, she observed how different she appeared from the other children who had arrived earlier in the evening. The exquisite young girl standing silently in front of her had no mask; she wore neither frightening makeup nor the lipstick Emily had seen used all night to mimic flowing blood on children's faces. Instead, she was dressed in a powder-blue dress, ankle-length stockings, and black patent leather shoes with black bows on the front. Her hair was jet black and cut into a Dutch bob with straight bangs that framed the symmetrical features of her smooth, alabaster face. Despite the fact that Emily had just recently moved into the apartment complex, she was certain she had seen the bulk of the youngsters come and go. However, she had not seen this one before. This one she would surely recall.

Emily realized after a few awkward seconds that neither of them had said anything. She had fully expected the traditional "trick or treat" to be shouted at her as she opened the door, but there was nothing but silence from this one. The silence became unsettling.

"Don't you think it's a little late for you to be out trick-or-treating?"

Since it was after 10 p.m., Emily cast a glance down the corridor, wondering where this child's parents were. The little girl stared up at her, motionless and silent.

"Sweetie? Do your parents know you're out this late?" she asked.

Still, the girl looked at her, expressionless.

Emily pressed, "Do you live on this floor? Can I walk you back home?"

The girl's demeanor slowly began to change, and she focused in on Emily with an intensity she'd never seen in someone so young.

"*You* don't belong here," hissed the little girl through clenched teeth, her tone quiet but menacing.

Emily was absolutely taken aback.

"I think you've gotten yourself all turned around, sweetie," Emily said. "How 'bout I walk you back to where you live?"

The little girl stood her ground, a smirk forming on her face.

"You're quite pretty," the girl whispered intensely. "But you'd better keep those pouty lips shut or you're gonna end up dead in the basement."

Emily recoiled but tried to remain composed. Suddenly, the little girl's face shifted to fear. "You'll end up like the rest of them!" the little girl said, pointing past Emily, into the apartment.

A chill crept over Emily as she looked over her shoulder and back into her apartment, half fearing she might actually see something.

"You're just another bitch like the other ones!"

Emily swung back around, horrified by what she'd just heard, but before she could speak, the girl dashed down the hall and around the corner, disappearing from view. Emily's first instinct was to run after her, but she paused and thought better of it, deciding instead not to engage in such disturbing behavior, whoever she was....

Her gaze was drawn to the shimmer of metal, no doubt from something the little girl had dropped. It was a small, heart-shaped locket, suspended from a chain. She bent down to pick it up and wondered if she should chase her down and hand it back to her.

She was already buzzed from the most recent beer she'd consumed, and it was past time for her to call it a night and retire to bed. She'd deal with it in the morning, when her mind was clearer. Besides, she thought, who would go running after some creepy little girl in the middle of the night? That never ended well in any of the movies she and Chloe used to stay up and watch together. She decided that Halloween was officially over as she pushed the door closed, making sure to latch the deadbolt.

4

The locket

"Hey Ted, I wanted to catch you up on my progress with the Jewelry store smash and grab story," Emily said, resting her desk phone on her shoulder and running her fingers over the notes her colleague had left for her to read. "This source you gave me couldn't confirm what was in the court records *and* she misidentified the suspect from the surveillance video capture you obtained from the store. *She* said it was her ex-boyfriend, so I ran his information, and he doesn't even live in the state anymore." Emily had become used to the frustration she'd sometimes elicit in her colleagues. As a fact-checker, she was frequently the bearer of bad news for a reporter who may have spent weeks developing the "perfect" angle for a story, only to be told they had to start over because the facts didn't match. Emily began again, "I really do think you have something here, but you're going to have to go at it another way." Emily noticed a copy of a receipt amongst the notes on her desk. "This receipt you gave me," Emily said, holding the paper closer to get a better look. "It's got a time and date stamp on it... this place has a camera over the register, and this Deli is next to the Jewelry store. Maybe try and see if the owners can match their footage up with the time stamp from this receipt? It's possible the guy who did the smash and grab used the deli, next door, to scope out the Jewelry store before he committed the crime. MmHmm, okay. Yeah. I'll talk to you later."

Emily hung up the phone and sat motionless, staring blankly into the monitor in front of her. She hadn't gotten much sleep at all, and she needed a break from her work. Her mind began to wander when her desk phone rang. She glanced at the caller ID; it was Chloe. Emily smiled and picked up the phone.

"Why are *you* calling me?" Emily teased.

"What do you mean, 'Why are *you* calling me'?" Chloe asked. "Is that *you* as in '*you* people'?"

"Oh, God. Here we go...."

"Don't be dissin' my ancestors!"

"Oh, don't be so high and mighty."

"Hey, 'Kaneko' is literally Japanese for 'golden child,'" Chloe said before bursting into laughter.

"Look, miss *golden child*, you work twenty-five feet from me. What's wrong? Are you getting lonely in your luxurious private office?" Emily could hear Chloe laughing, both through the phone and from across the hall with her other ear.

"I got bored and thought I'd see how the other half lives. What's life like out there in the bullpen?"

"It's loud and everyone keeps trying to get in my business, you little shit! Don't you have something better to do?"

"I wanted to see how the big search was going.... *Nancy Drew and the Case of the Stolen Diamond!*"

"It's a locket and chain, dumb-ass. And, no, I'm not any closer to finding who it belongs to."

"Why don't you just give up, then? Finder's keepers!"

"Honestly? I'd kind of like to meet that girl's mother, see what *she's* like. I mean, who'd let their kid out without any supervision at all, that late at night?"

"Um, I don't know, maybe anyone who's ever spent any time with a kid? Actually, you know what? I think you're right. Find the mom, and then maybe you could get some fashion tips from her."

Emily waited for Chloe to stop cackling at her own joke. "You'd like that, wouldn't you?"

"No, but I'd bet Peter would…."

"Shut up!"

"All dressed up in your little dress…and your patent leather shoes and knee-high stockings…."

"Shut. The fuck. Up!" said Emily through clenched teeth, trying to suppress a laugh.

"Has he asked you out yet?"

"No, why?"

"He's going to…."

She could practically feel Chloe's teasing smile through the phone. Emily had developed a small crush on Peter, the 6pm news producer, within the first week of starting her new job in the office, and she made the mistake of mentioning that fact to Chloe. Truth be told, it felt exciting that Peter might be interested in her. Emily felt secure that if Peter had Chloe's seal of approval, he was "one of the good ones." Still, she wasn't going to encourage Chloe's teasing a moment longer where that subject was concerned.

"Do you have anything useful to tell me? Any idea what I

should do to return the locket?"

"Are you any closer to figuring out who owns it?"

"No, but the last week or so, I've been asking total strangers in the halls if they have a little girl with a Dutch bob haircut. Maybe I should just give it to the landlord."

"Knock, knock, knock! Hey! Nancy Drew! How are you supposed to see who the locket belongs to? Don't give it to the landlord!"

"You got a better idea, Sherlock?"

"Have you tried putting a sign in the lobby? 'Discovered… Locket and Chain. Contact Emily Pierson in apartment 307.'"

"Of course, I tried that. I'm not an idiot. All *that* managed to do was bring people out of the woodwork to meet 'the new girl'!"

Emily paused for a moment, then looked at the time. "I should probably get back to what I was doing. Talk later?"

"Sure. Oh, remind me later to talk to you about my idea for you."

"Okay…talk soon."

Emily had only just hung up when she was confronted with a mountain of notes to review and a looming deadline. It would be a long day.

* * *

That evening, Emily returned home, numb from the day. Getting a piece on the news that she'd had a hand in used to feel so exciting. But lately, it just felt like another day. Still, it was going to be another major story for tonight's six o'clock broadcast, a piece on a local city council member who embezzled city funds, not half bad for the new girl at WROC

Channel 8.

She stepped into the lobby, where she removed the notecard she'd placed earlier in the week in the hope of finding the owner of the locket. She'd all but given up the search at this point, and she was too tired to think of much else but to go upstairs, draw a bath, and pour herself a glass of wine.

Turning to the elevator, she heard a weak voice ask her to hold the elevator door open. Emily placed her palm along the elevator door's opening to keep the retracted door from closing and turned to see who had spoken to her. An older lady with her white hair neatly put into a bun entered the elevator. She greeted Emily with a smile and stood alongside her as the elevator door closed in front of them.

"Many thanks, dear," the woman remarked quietly as she raised her eyes to Emily. Then she shifted her attention to the changing numbers above the elevator door. Emily returned the woman's courteous smile before also nervously focusing her eyes on the elevator floor numbers.

"Which floor are you on?" Emily inquired, gesturing with her finger toward the buttons on the elevator panel.

"Oh, sweetheart, we share a floor," the old woman responded with slight amusement.

"Oh? I apologize. I'm still figuring out how to navigate the building and becoming acquainted with everyone."

"I live across the hall and a few doors down from you." The woman peeked at the index card Emily was holding, smiled, and then returned her gaze. "Any news about the locket?" she asked.

Emily smiled as she looked down at the card and responded, slightly dejected, "No."

"I might have some ideas. May I see the locket?" the woman

asked.

"Of course," Emily said, with just a hint of hesitancy. "It's in my apartment."

Once on the third floor, the elevator came to a standstill and paused before gently opening into the corridor. They walked down the hall together, Emily tripping slightly as she attempted to keep to a slower pace with the woman.

"I'm right here," Emily said, pointing to her door. She struggled with her key before unlocking it and allowing it to swing open the remainder of the way as she invited the woman into her apartment.

"Excuse me for a moment. Please have a seat. I'll be right back," Emily said as she dashed down the hallway to her bedroom to grab the locket.

Emily quickly returned to the front room and discovered the woman seated comfortably on the couch.

"My name is Hazel, by the way."

"Pleased to meet you, Hazel," said Emily before introducing herself.

Emily extended her hand with the chain dangling from her fingers to Hazel and then sat alongside her. They both fixed their gaze on the locket. Hazel carefully removed it from Emily's fingers, gradually taking up the remainder of the chain as she inspected the locket, turning it over to expose the writing on the back. Emily watched the woman read the words to herself, her mouth quietly articulating each word as her eyes traveled across the engraving.

Dearest Myra,
You Are Always in My Heart.
L.P. Brooks

Emily watched as Hazel flipped the locket back over and a grin formed on the old woman's lips. She couldn't wait to ask, "Is it yours?"

"Oh, my goodness, no, dear," Hazel replied softly.

"Can you tell me anything about it?" Emily asked.

"Yes, I suppose I can."

"I'm so glad to hear that," Emily said."

"This first initial, 'L,' stands for Leonard. This was a gift from Leonard Brooks to his wife, Myra. After they passed, the locket was given to their eldest daughter. She was an old neighbor of mine who used to live in this building."

Emily wasn't sure what to make of all that she was hearing, least of all how any of this connected to the little girl she had met on Halloween. She was beginning to suspect that the young girl had either stolen it or just discovered it and decided to keep it for herself. But where would the girl have found it?

Hazel proceeded, "I looked after her when she became unable to care for herself, and over time, I guess we became pretty close friends — as close as she'd allow, anyway. She could be pretty full of vim and vigor a lot of the time. I guess I don't blame her. She was in a lot of pain at the end of her life."

Emily listened attentively.

After a pause, Hazel said, "I'm so sorry, dear. I just realized that I haven't told you who I'm talking about."

Emily shook her head, smiling politely.

"Well, if you were as old as I am, you'd probably know her by name or at the very least by that hair style she had when she was young."

Hazel paused again.

"Can you believe that I used to care for a world-famous Hollywood film actress?"

Emily perked up a bit. Hazel's reference to a once-famous person provided an intriguing twist to the mystery.

"Please tell me you've heard of Charlie Chaplin or Greta Garbo, dear," Hazel teased.

"Yes, of course, I've heard of them."

"Well, the woman I'm referring to had affairs with both of 'em!"

Emily grabbed her laptop and pulled it closer.

"Now who was it you say used to live here?" asked Emily, opening her browser with her fingers poised, ready to begin typing.

"Louise Brooks," responded Hazel as she watched Emily type the search terms into the search bar.

"Louise Brooks," 1920's film actress…

Emily was transfixed as her screen filled with references and images. The black-and-white image of a woman from an era long passed stared back at her. She was incredibly beautiful, and her appearance seemed quite contemporary. The woman in the photos wore her jet-black hair in a bob, cut short at her ears with the dark pointed tips cutting into her alabaster cheeks, perfectly framing her dark, sultry eyes. The straight lines of her blunt bangs were the ideal accent to her stick-straight brows, and her perfect lips curved in just enough of a pout to seem sad yet inviting.

Emily had no clue that women in the 1920s could look like this. The flappers she had seen in photographs from that era did not resemble this woman at all. They wore their hair in curls, and they looked almost comical — like Betty Boop.

For Emily, the woman's appearance was completely hypnotic. At this point, one image in particular struck Emily's eye. The faded picture of a little girl standing outside, next to a chair. Emily focused her concentration even more and clicked on the image, enlarging it to fill her laptop screen. Emily's mind began to swirl. The little girl in the photograph looked like the young girl she had seen on Halloween night. Emily's eyes then shifted down, toward the caption at the bottom of the photograph.

Louise Brooks, age 9, on the front porch of her
family's home in Cherryvale, Kansas, 1915.

"As I told you, dear, Louise Brooks hasn't lived in this building for a very long time, and she died before you were even born." Hazel surveyed the room, then added, "She lived here, in *your* apartment."

"My apartment? Wait, did that caption say Cherryvale, Kansas?" Emily said, incredulously; she felt goosebumps on her arms at the odds that she and anyone else from Cherryvale would end up in the same apartment.

Hazel nodded, then scooted herself forward in order to give herself enough leverage to push herself up from the couch, and Emily held out her hand to take the woman's arm and help her the rest of the way.

"I'm sure your little girl must have picked up that locket somewhere in the building. I can't imagine there's much, but I suppose some of Louise's belongings may still be in storage down in the basement."

Hazel looked down and began to shake her head. "Poor thing. I guess nobody ever even came to claim the last of her things."

Emily moved to the door and opened it, assisting Hazel through the doorway. Hazel paused and looked up at Emily once more.

"You watch after that locket, darling," Hazel said, then shuffled down the hall to her own apartment.

Emily watched her new friend until she was sure Hazel had gotten into her own apartment safely. Then she shut her own door and locked it. As she surveyed her surroundings with a fresh new perspective, she smiled, and in that brief moment, she even entertained the thought of getting her own hair chopped to a fashionable bob with straight bangs.

5

Revelations and More Questions

Emily was ecstatic to tell Chloe about the new information she'd discovered about the locket — and its connection to the little girl — the following day at work. While Emily had kept Chloe informed of the locket mystery on a daily basis, she had always been careful not to tell her about the more disturbing aspects of her late-night encounter with the young girl at her door weeks earlier. The unsettling nature of their conversation was more than Emily felt comfortable disclosing to another person. It was simply too strange.

With this new information about the former tenant of the apartment she was now occupying, Emily felt compelled to tell Chloe everything.

She'd trusted Chloe enough to share the reasons that had led to her abrupt departure from New York; surely, she could divulge *this* story, about her possibly having encountered the ghost of an old Hollywood star. She was certain that everyone

— except Chloe — would dismiss this story as ridiculous.

Chloe stood attentively by her friend, her straight black hair falling on Emily's shoulder as she typed in the search words she'd input the previous night at home.

Chloe moved closer to the monitor as Emily began to look up images on her computer. "Are you shitting me, Em?"

Emily smiled back at her. "Nope. That's her, Louise Brooks, the silent film star who used to live in my apartment."

"I actually recognize her."

"Yeah, I did, too, but I had no idea what her name was."

Chloe shook her head. "No, me neither…."

Emily smiled and watched as her friend took it all in. Chloe took the mouse from Emily and began scrolling through more images.

"Holy shit, she's stunning!" Chloe exclaimed. "Hell, I'd do her." Chloe turned to Emily and continued, pointing at the image on the screen, "So *she*… lived in *your* apartment?"

Emily nodded.

"Why?" said Chloe.

"I honestly have no clue. Hazel told me she'd been a recluse for the last thirty years of her life." Emily paused and thought a little bit more on it. "So why would a woman like that, someone who was called…what was that…hang on." She took back the mouse and clicked on a link to another website. "Here we go." Emily continued, pointing her finger at a headline on the screen, "Why would a woman who was called 'the most sensual image ever committed to celluloid' end up a recluse, living in that small apartment…here in Rochester?"

"I don't know, but this sounds like a great local interest piece," said Chloe.

Gazing up at her friend, Emily could see that Chloe's on-air persona had taken over. It didn't help that she had no time to change out of her blazer and pencil skirt after she'd done the morning news.

"Mmm, I don't know."

"Are you kidding? Why the hell not?"

"Well, I haven't told you everything." Emily's body tightened.

"What? What is it?"

Emily clicked on another screen image to enlarge the photo.

"So?" Chloe said.

"Read the caption," Emily said.

Chloe read aloud, "Louise Brooks, age 9, on the front porch of her family's home in Cherryvale, Kansas, 1915."

Chloe looked up at Emily. "That's your hometown, isn't it?"

"Yes, and that's the girl," Emily answered, pointing at the image on the screen.

"What girl?"

Emily became more emphatic. "That's who knocked on my door on Halloween night!"

Chloe's eyes widened, struggling with the information she just received.

"No, it isn't."

Emily nodded. "Yes…it is. And I'm not just saying there's a resemblance. I'm telling you that *she*…" Emily pointed again at the image and continued, "*that exact girl* in *that photo* showed up at my front door on Halloween night."

"Are you saying you saw a ghost or something?" Chloe asked.

"I don't know what I'm saying," Emily said, shaking her head. "I know, it sounds insane, but I'm telling you, it was her. She wasn't like some see-through, blurry glowing person or anything like you see in movies. She was solid — she was as real as you or me!"

Chloe now understood the seriousness of what Emily was conveying to her, and she brought her hand gently to Emily's arm. "You're trembling."

Emily began to tear up.

"Em, look. It's okay," Chloe said in a softer tone.

Emily began to break down. "It's what she said to me."

"I know, you told me that already," Chloe said. "She called you a 'bitch.'"

After a long silence, Chloe tried to break the tension. Grinning sheepishly, Chloe added "She's not wrong, you know."

Emily continued, unable to contain her emotions, the stress of keeping this bottled up now flooding forth. "She told me I didn't belong there…"

Chloe pulled Emily into her arms.

With one final release, Emily let the rest of it out. "Then she told me that I was pretty, but if I didn't keep my mouth shut, I'd end up dead in the basement…*like the others.*"

Chloe continued to hold Emily. "Oh, my God. No wonder you've been so stressed out lately."

"I've been wanting to tell someone, anyone, since it happened. But who would believe me?" Emily cried, still quivering; she sat back down.

Chloe then looked around to get a read on the rest of the room. One or two coworkers were staring at the two of them, but they weren't near enough that they could hear any of the conversation to this point.

"Look, I'm going to come over to your place tonight after work," Chloe said, looking into Emily's now bloodshot eyes. "Okay?"

Emily nodded her head. Then Chloe looked over at the few

who were still staring. "Hey! Numb nuts! Take a picture. it'll last longer!"

It worked. The two onlookers turned back to their work, and Emily was able to regain her composure.

Emily looked up at Chloe, and they both began to laugh. She felt relieved that Chloe could now be her confidante for this unbelievably weird problem as well.

"You know what you need?" said Chloe, swiveling Emily's chair back to face her. "Remember yesterday, I told you there was an idea I was gonna talk to you about?"

Emily began to shake her head.

"You can't say no because we're doin' it!" Chloe said. She pointed up at her temple and continued, "I've already got it all planned up here."

"You've got *what* planned?" asked Emily.

"We're gonna have a housewarming get-together for you. We're gonna invite a few people from work…."

"Yeah? Can you invite Peter?"

"Absolutely!"

"Well, good. That settles that," said Emily definitely. She could feel the butterflies flitting around in her stomach at the mere mention of his name, but she continued to play it cool.

"And it's gonna be a roaring twenties theme!"

"Hard NO," said Emily.

"Okay, okay! But I'm not taking any lip from the likes of you on anything else. Oh, and you should invite Hazel! She can be our 'something old.'" Chloe burst out laughing.

"It's not a wedding, doofus."

"Whatever," said Chloe. "We're doin' this thing!"

6

Mary, Mary Quite Contrary

She'd had the run of the house for as long as she could remember. There was only one steadfast rule at home: Don't bother your father. Not that she would ever have to; the house was full of books and music. So many delights at hand to fill her day. In the adjacent room, her mother could be heard performing a concerto by Claude Debussy on the piano. Mary adored listening to her mother play, and her mother relished the opportunity to watch her precocious little lamb dance.

However, something else had captured Mary's attention that day. Martin, her older brother, was headed out to Lake Tanko, a local lake about a mile from their home, and she was not about to be left out. All of the Brooks children loved to fish and swim at the lake.

"Hey, wait up," she yelled at her brother, who had walked well beyond the front porch and was already halfway across the street.

"That's enough caterwauling," her mother said, irritated at the break in her concentration. "If you're going to behave like a monkey,

just go outside with your brother!"

Her mother watched from the piano, a look of exasperation on her face, as her daughter, another one of her four children, raced across the wood floor and through the front door. Then she returned to her piece, running her finger along the sheet music to reestablish her place in the composition.

From the porch, Mary couldn't see Martin, but she knew the route down to the lake. She was unaccustomed to traveling that far alone, but she wasn't going to be left behind. As she ran down the street, she could hear the music of Debussy begin again behind her.

Several blocks from the house, Mary slowed to a walk. She had started to suspect that Martin was not going to the lake after all. She should have been able to see him in the distance, but she couldn't. She came to a halt, enraged that her brother hadn't waited for her. She looked back toward her house, but the view was obstructed by trees and other homes.

She decided she'd head back home, but something else piqued her interest. The elderly gentleman who occasionally performed odd jobs for her parents sat on the porch of a nearby house, eating a sandwich. His gaze followed her every step as she walked past the house across the street, down the dirt path that ran along the front of the house.

"Where you off to, cupcake?" asked the man, pausing to finish chewing a mouthful of his sandwich.

She came to a halt and shifted her weight onto the heels of her scuffed, black Mary Janes. She was wise enough not to approach an adult without being invited.

The man set down what was left of his sandwich and reached into the pocket of his paint-stained overalls with his other hand.

"Do you like candy?" he asked.

She nodded. The man removed a cloth from his pocket and

unwrapped it, revealing several pieces of hard candy.

"All right, c'mon over now," he said impatiently. Then he smiled a toothy, disgusting grin, and called to her again, "I ain't gonna bite."

The man laid the open cloth down beside him on the porch and then patted the wood as one might do to entice a stray dog to come closer.

She cast one final glance back to see if she could see Martin in the distance. She couldn't. Then she took her first tentative steps toward the treats.

7

Sanctuary

A few days had passed since Emily had confided in Chloe about the unusual circumstances that had occurred in her apartment building. It was late Autumn, and the days were growing shorter. Emily loved this time of year, particularly the crispness in the air as the nights grew colder.

She entered the apartment after work and turned on the small table lamp closest to the door. As she surveyed the warmly lit corners of her apartment's main room, she breathed deeply and smiled. Home at last. Since she'd come clean to Chloe about her brush with the paranormal, it had been long enough for her fear to fade. Nothing out of the ordinary had happened since Halloween, so she felt secure returning home after work to her empty apartment, even after dark. Notwithstanding the unpleasant aura that had briefly enveloped the space weeks previously, Emily's apartment remained her favorite place to withdraw into quiet introspection, which never failed to reenergize her, especially after a full day at work in the bullpen.

Emily raised her eyes to the little clock she'd put on the wall of her open kitchen, relieved that she'd arrived home early enough to recover with a hot bath before Chloe would arrive for their Tuesday "girls' night."

She wasted no time in getting started, kicking off her heels as she walked to the bathroom and began unbuttoning her blouse. Once inside, she started to fill the tub, checking to ensure the water was at the desired temperature. She stretched herself over the tub to light a trio of multitiered candles she'd placed on a corner bathroom shelf, then added some bath beads and watched as a layer of soft, bubbling suds began to build on the water. The scent of jasmine wafted through the air. She turned her gaze to the bathroom mirror, raising her hair in the back and securing it with one of her large hair clips. She slipped out of her final piece of clothing, dropping it onto the pile on the tile floor next to the tub, and slid into the warm, welcoming safe place she'd created for herself underneath all those suds.

To most people, even those who worked with her, Emily seemed outgoing. Indeed, she had honed this skill through years of practice to the point that it had evolved into a sort of second skin — a carefully honed persona — that she could don whenever the situation warranted it and that she wore effortlessly while out with others. The reality that she was an introvert was known to only a few of her closest friends. Naturally, Alex was aware, as was Chloe. The reality was that she often found spending time with other people exhausting. Time like this — time spent alone with no cell phone, no TV noise, no bright lights — this was Nirvana for her.

Emily's body relaxed in the warm, soothing water. Her stresses from the day melted away as she sank further into the water. Her mind began to wander, sifting random moments as they flashed briefly into her head. For a brief moment, she could see Alex beaming back at her, a fragment of a memory from months before, on New Year's Eve. They were slow dancing, and she was reminded of how beautiful everything seemed in that moment.

She was nostalgic for the good times with Alex more than ever. Though it had been only a few months since she left, Emily had established enough geographical — and emotional — distance from Alex to forget how upset she had been with him. She'd even begun to doubt her impulsive decision to leave so abruptly and especially while he was still at work. Looking back now at her actions in the moment, she felt silly for having overreacted as she did and making so many assumptions about Alex's behavior. She began to wonder if she should have confronted Alex and given him an opportunity to explain himself. Perhaps he'd had a perfectly reasonable explanation for his behavior and for working late so frequently. And it's not as if he'd made no attempt to contact her after she left; she still had several missed calls and messages from him on her phone which she'd ignored. Now she wished that she had at least answered the phone. She still lacked the courage to delete his messages which suggested she still couldn't let go completely.

Emily knew that in his frustration with not being able to find her, Alex had spoken to her mother, primarily to ensure that she was safe and that she was with family or friends she could rely on during her absence from him. Emily's mother informed her that Alex was adamant that he would not abandon their relationship, that there was nothing wrong, and that if given the opportunity to speak with her, he could explain everything. Despite Emily's feelings, her mother still trusted Alex. When she informed Emily of their phone call, she stated that she instinctively knew he was telling the truth, insisting that it was her "mother's intuition," and since Emily trusted her mother's judgement, she was now reconsidering her refusal to talk to Alex.

Emily began to believe that returning at least one of Alex's calls would not be the worst thing in the world. She made a mental note to herself that if he phoned again, as she now hoped he would, she would answer and speak with him. She chuckled at herself and understood at that moment that being alone with her thoughts, soothed by the warm glow of a few candles, and being able to unwind for the first time in days had served as a potent motivator, even prompting her to inevitably rethink her rejection of Alex.

As the candlelight flickered, Emily's thoughts drifted. Her first intimate encounter with Alex surged through her head. Transported back to that night, she felt the anticipation of his touch. She began to tremble, and her heart pounded. She flushed from head to toe.

She envisioned Alex's hand working its way up her thigh when, instantly, another vision burst into focus. Alex's hand transformed into a slightly darker, more calloused hand roughly grabbing at her thigh. She could hear a low, gravelly voice that she didn't recognize but that seemed sickeningly familiar. She could see the man's other hand grab her hip as he threw her to the cold floor of a darkened cellar. A musty smell filled her nostrils as she scrabbled to get away.

The buzzer on the intercom panel next to the front door

sounded, jolting Emily from the dark vision. She lurched out of the tub, splashing water onto the floor, wrapped a towel around herself, and raced to the door.

"It's me, Em," said Chloe through the speaker. "Hurry up. It's cold out here."

Emily buzzed her up. Although Chloe's early arrival cut short Emily's bath, she was grateful that it had erased the vision of the basement from her mind.

Chloe burst through the door, a bottle of wine in hand.

"What's with the peep show?" she asked, smiling at Emily's half-naked, wet body. "You're not expecting me to leave a wad of cash on your nightstand when I leave, are you?"

"Shut up," Emily retorted while smiling, running back to her bedroom to dry off and put on some clothes. "Make yourself at home."

"Always do," replied Chloe, removing her coat and throwing it over the back of a chair.

From her bedroom, Emily could hear the sound from the TV come on; she smiled, wondering how it was that the two of them ever managed to keep such a tight friendship given their completely different personalities. As within any symbiotic relationship, however, they were the perfect odd couple.

"What do you want on your pizza, Em?" Chloe shouted from the outer room.

"Ham and sausage," Emily answered, removing the hair clip and letting her hair fall back into place. She pulled on her sweats.

Emily finally came out of the bedroom and plopped herself onto the couch. Chloe had already opened a bottle of red, filled two glasses, and placed them on the coffee table in front of the couch.

"So, I did some digging around on our Miss Brooks," said Chloe, seating herself next to Emily. "Apparently, she was more than just a total smokeshow. I read somewhere that she was given credit for being one of the first actors to use a more realistic style of acting."

"Oh, yeah?"

"You know how actors from the early days were so dramatic, how they used that waving-your-arms-about kind of acting style? When Louise came on the scene, what she did was so different that they didn't even recognize what she was doing as acting at all. From what I read, when audiences watch her performances now, they see that she stands out as the only person in the scene who appears to behave like a normal person. Not like some fucking spaz."

Chloe took a sip of her drink and leapt off the couch, gripping her throat as though she had just been poisoned, and sticking her tongue out dramatically. Emily watched her friend fall to the floor in front of the coffee table, like someone in a silent comedy.

Emily spit up the wine she'd just taken into her mouth. "You freak!" she exclaimed, laughing.

At that moment, they heard three distinct thuds and felt the floor shudder.

"Sorry!" Emily yelled, directing her voice down at her neighbor on the second floor.

The two looked at each other and burst into laughter again.

They settled into watching the TV while they waited for the pizza to arrive.

"We should watch her sometime," Emily said, breaking the silence. "You know, one of her films."

Chloe nodded, not taking her gaze off the TV. Emily pulled

up a search engine on her phone and began looking for Louise Brooks film titles.

"It looks like the film she's most known for is *Pandora's Box*." Emily continued to slide her finger across her phone, scrolling from item to item before stopping on something that caught her attention.

"According to the Criterion Collection liner notes, that's the one to watch," said Emily as she began to read to herself.

Chloe broke her gaze from the TV and turned to Emily, watching her as she continued to read the text from her phone.

"Is it available to stream?" asked Chloe, picking up the remote and preparing to punch in the appropriate streaming channel.

"It is," said Emily, squinting her eyes, and pulling the phone closer to her face. "Just go to "search" and it should pop up."

As they searched for and located the film title, the pizza arrived. Chloe went down to the lobby to pick it up and tip the delivery guy while Emily readied the coffee table with plates and napkins.

For the rest of the evening, Emily and Chloe watched their first Louise Brooks film, intermittently stopping to refill their wine glasses.

Emily sat riveted by the woman who had once lived where she and Chloe now sat, transfixed by the woman's beauty and occasionally downright wicked come-hither stares as her character, Lulu, decimated those who dared attempt to possess her, if only fleetingly.

Emily savored the feeling of peace, enjoying the calm that had enveloped them both. When Chloe arrived earlier in the evening, it was Emily's intention for them to eat, drink and talk to their hearts' content, thus providing each other with much needed company until Chloe was too tired to go home. As Emily looked over at Chloe, who was beginning to fall asleep, she decided that they had indeed accomplished what they had set out to do this night.

Emily leaned over and nudged Chloe, "I think you'd better stay the night; it's too late to go home now, and you've had too much wine."

They helped each other up from the couch, turned off the TV, and switched off the lights on their way back to Emily's bedroom, flopping themselves onto the mattress. They each took a piece of the bed's top sheet and blanket and pulled it over them. By the time their heads struck the pillows, relaxed and tired form the wine and conversation, they were quick to pass out.

Later in the evening, Emily was awakened by something gently tugging at the bottom of the bedcover. As she opened her eyes, she could now see that the sheet was slowly being dragged down toward her feet. She looked at Chloe, about to tell her to stop hogging the covers, but Chloe was still asleep. Emily jerked up, yanking the cord on her bedside table lamp, flooding the room with light. The sheet was now still. There was nothing there but her and Chloe. A moment later, Chloe felt the chill air on her legs and groggily reached for the blanket, pulling it back over her body before sleepily muttering, "too much light." Emily shut off the light and pulled the blanket fast around her shoulders, pinning it in place to prevent any movement.

8

The housewarming

Another week passed. It was finally Friday evening — the night of Emily's housewarming party. The arrival of the event eased Emily's nerves somewhat. There was no time left to do anything but welcome the guests.

Hazel was the first to arrive. She told Emily she was just being "fashionably early." Emily didn't mind; she enjoyed Hazel's company, and she'd become ever more comfortable asking Hazel about her friendship with Louise. Shortly thereafter, several of her coworkers arrived, and the party was well underway.

Emily was deep in conversation with Hazel when she heard Peter's voice at the front door. He was greeted by some of Emily's other coworkers.

Finally, Chloe made her own grand entrance, bearing a gift, an exquisitely framed enlargement of a photograph of Louise Brooks taken in 1929 by famed photographer Eugene

Robert Richee. Louise wore a silk kimono in the photograph, her elbow resting on the arm of the chair she was sitting in. Her head was cocked to one side, and she gazed off into the distance. Perhaps most instantly recognizable in the photo was her signature hairstyle, jet-black bobbed hair and bangs, perfectly framing her facial features.

"She was so beautiful," said Hazel, gazing up at the print under glass. "Where did you find this, Chloe?"

Emily glanced at Hazel. She winked back at Emily with a smile, then winked, as if she already knew something about the print.

"Oh my God, you guys," Chloe began excitedly as she addressed both Hazel and Emily. "I literally spent this whole week devising the ideal present for Emily's new apartment. It turns out I can do a little fact checking myself."

Emily smiled as she watched her friend carry on.

"I read that the Louise Brooks collection was held at Rochester's historic Eastman house museum," Chloe continued. "So I made a few calls and found out that the museum gift shop contained limited edition reproductions of some of Louise Brooks' most exquisite Hollywood portraits and publicity stills. On my lunch break, I paid a visit to the museum and picked out the one I thought would be the most striking image of Louise."

"I'd say you pretty much nailed it, Chloe," said Emily, still very much stunned at such a grand gesture.

"I thought it would be the perfect complement to your new apartment," answered Chloe, "and it would go well with your Art Deco sensibility. Once I saw it in its matte black frame, I couldn't wait to see the look on your face tonight."

Emily hugged Chloe and thanked her again for such a thoughtful gift. Then Chloe dashed across the room with the framed print.

"Have you got a hammer and a hook, Em?" asked Chloe, holding the print up on this wall and then another.

"There should be something in the drawer by the sink," muttered Emily as she opened the drawer and began to rummage through it. "Got it," she called out to Chloe.

Chloe responded, "Where do you want me to hang this, Em? It's heavy. Pick a wall!"

Chloe looked over at Peter and motioned him over to her. "Come help me hang this over here, tall, dark, and handy."

"How much have you had to drink?" asked Peter, giving Chloe a nudge, and then laughing at her.

"Em!" yelled Chloe. "What are you doing? Come *over* here and defend my honor! Peter's accusing me of being a lush!" Emily smiled, handing the hammer and hook to Chloe. Chloe and Peter stumbled around, trying to hang the print.

When he put the hammer down, Peter glanced over and focused his gaze upon Emily. She wore a burnt-orange boatneck sweater and form-fitting jeans, a combination she hoped would help her stand out. From Peter's expression, it obviously had worked.

The intercom buzzed again. It was her coworker, Gina. Emily pressed the intercom button and instructed Gina to come up.

In a few minutes, Gina and her two girls stepped in, closing and locking the door behind them.

"Sorry for the 'plus two,'" Gina said. "My ex was being a prick, so change of plans. I hope it's okay."

"Of course, it is," said Emily, helping her friend settle the two little ones in her bedroom. Gina had thought enough to bring along the kids' backpacks with some paper and crayons that they could use to draw with, and Emily offered the two some juice to hold them over. Closing the door to the bedroom, Emily guided Gina to the kitchen, offering her friend a beer.

As the evening wore on, and Emily watched her friends and coworkers mingle, she reveled in the laughter and frivolity that seemed to transform the space. Emily smiled and watched her friends, focusing on each conversation, and she thought to herself that she hadn't felt this content in some time. Across the room, she caught Peter's eye, and he smiled at her. Emily smiled back. He side-stepped his way around some of Emily's other coworkers, who were sitting on the floor, made his way to Emily, and stood beside her.

"I thought I should come over and tell you how much I love your place," he said.

"Thanks," Emily said.

They stood side by side, awkwardly surveying the room and guests.

"Thanks for inviting me, by the way," Peter said, looking down at his beer, then taking another sip.

"No, I mean, yeah, no, really, it's my pleasure," Emily replied, looking up to meet Peter's eyeline. "Chloe said you two have worked together for a while now."

"Yep... yep. She's really great," Peter said, looking down at Emily.

"Why are we talking about Chloe, anyway?" said Emily, not quite sure why it even came out of her mouth, "we should be talking more about how you like to hammer random girls'... walls."

Surprised, he choked on his beer. Feeling unusually emboldened by a spirit of confident sexuality, she grinned and stepped closer to Peter, her eyes darting about to take in every detail of his face before settling on his lips. Pulling him into the hallway a bit more, she lifted one arm to lay her hand on his chest and the other to wrap her hand behind his neck. Tilting her head back, she raised her gaze to his and eventually took in his soft lips. Peter drew his mouth in closer. Emily began gently caressing his lips with hers; then she slipped her tongue inside his mouth, an act that was completely out of character for her, since she was never this forward with anybody, let alone someone she hardly knew. Peter put his hands on her hips, pulled her against him, and kissed her passionately.

Chloe was across the room, speaking with another of their friends, when she noticed Peter and Emily up against the wall in an embrace. Chloe raised her eyebrows, clearly surprised by their display in view of everyone, yet shifted her gaze back to her conversation.

* * *

Later into the evening, Chloe moved from the couch over to the refrigerator to grab another chilled bottle of chardonnay. With her back to the kitchen counter, Emily leaned toward Chloe.

"How do you think it's going?" Emily asked in a whisper.

"I think it's a hit," Chloe said, "Why? Don't you?"

"Yeah, I guess it is."

Emily moved her empty glass over to Chloe so she could get a refill.

"What do you think Peter thinks of the party?" Emily asked, watching Chloe pouring more wine into her glass.

"I'm guessing Peter thinks the party is great," Chloe said. "*You* of all people should know he's enjoying himself, Miss Kissy-Face."

Emily closed her eyes as she winced. "Oh, no. Did everybody see that?"

"No, just me. Everyone else was gabbing away about their own stuff, too busy to be watching you two," said Chloe. "By the way, what was up with that?"

"What do you mean?"

"Pretty bold move, jumping Peter like you did. Since when are you all about the PDA?"

"Huh," Emily said, shaking her head. "I really don't know."

Emily took a brief pause. Chloe was right; that was not *her*.

"I don't know. Maybe a wave of confidence came over me. I felt attractive and powerful, things I never really feel. Weird."

Emily had kept herself closed off for most of her life, particularly when it came to her sexual self. While most of her classmates were embarking on their first adventures, attending dances, group dating, and the like, Emily lacked the confidence to seek any activity that would push her into such an encounter. Outsiders regarded her as withdrawn and sad to be around.

By high school, Emily's solitary image had become more firmly entrenched, a demeanor that alienated most people. Emily had thought a lot about her personality in the years since she left Cherryvale, back when she was in high school, and viewed it as a kind of subconscious self-preservation.

Emily turned her attention to the framed print of Louise on the wall, and for a moment, she felt envious of how sexually confident Louise had seemed to be in all of her publicity photos, a feeling Emily had fleetingly experienced in the hallway with Peter.

"I really do appreciate the gift," she said to Chloe.

"Yeah, it's cool," Chloe said, as she turned around and leaned against the counter beside Emily, pulling her phone from her pocket. "Let's take a selfie to commemorate this night!"

The two of them looked up at the phone Chloe held out in front of them and quickly transformed their expressions into their perfect selfie poses.

"Text them to me!" laughed Emily.

"Of course," answered Chloe. "Just let me edit them and run them through some of my filters."

Chloe smiled and winked at Emily as she made her way back over to the floor to sit with one of their coworkers. Emily smiled back at her and decided she should embrace the fun. Swallowing the rest of her wine, she grabbed another chilled bottle of chardonnay and then carefully stepped her way through the guests seated on the floor and sat down next to Peter, topping off his wine glass.

* * *

Eventually, all of Emily's guests except Chloe and Hazel said their farewells. Chloe had planned to stay the night again, which was good since she was in no position to drive.

Emily looked over at Hazel, who was gathering her purse and her coat, and she thought to herself what a cool woman Hazel turned out to be; she'd outlasted practically all of the other guests at the party.

Hazel shuffled over to Emily and reached forward to grasp her arm. She leaned into Emily and smiled.

"Have you seen our little Lulu again, dear?" Hazel asked in a whispering tone.

Emily felt an uneasy flash of recognition. "Little Lulu," she repeated flatly. "Little…Louise?"

Hazel didn't acknowledge the question. "I'm certain she'll return, my dear," she said. "She always does."

Hazel patted Emily's arm as she began walking toward the

door, her purse dangling from her other arm. Emily grew even more uncomfortable with the acknowledgement that Hazel, too, had seen Louise's ghost.

Hazel added, "She's paid me several visits over the years."

Hazel winked at Emily, then pushed her way through the doorway and down the outer hallway to her apartment, leaving Emily speechless. Emily's mind raced as she closed the door, pushing the deadbolt to lock it. Then she turned and slumped against the door. Hazel, she now realized, had known the little girl's identity all along.

* * *

Emily was exhausted but still buzzing from the wine — and the revelation from Hazel. She figured that she should probably clean up, or at the very least collect the glasses and dishes and place them into the sink, so she wouldn't have quite as much to deal with the following morning.

"Fuck it," she murmured to herself as she collapsed onto the couch next to Chloe, who had just switched on the TV.

Emily recalled the selfies Chloe had taken of them earlier that evening.

"Chloe, let me see your phone."

"What do you want?" Chloe asked, sounding drowsy.

"I wanna see the pics you took tonight."

Chloe handed Emily her phone.

"The password is my birthday," Chloe explained, adding with a laugh, "and don't delete any of the dick pics!"

Emily rolled her eyes and began scrolling through Chloe's pictures before stopping on the selfies they took.

"Wow," exclaimed Emily with a laugh. "You're right about

needing to add some filters."

"Let me see," said Chloe, pulling her phone closer.

"I look horrible!" said Emily.

"You're fine," Chloe said dismissively. "I just need to undo the 'whore' filter I already added on you."

Emily playfully poked her elbow into Chloe's side, and they both began laughing. It was obvious they both needed to get some sleep.

Emily continued scrolling to the following image. It was a shot from across the room, directed toward a couple of Emily and Chloe's coworkers. Emily grinned, her mind absorbed in another memory from earlier that evening.

"Hey, googly eyes, give me my phone back," remarked Chloe, who was feeling a little cheeky at the moment.

Emily handed the phone to Chloe and closed her eyes, resting her head on the back of the couch.

She thought about what Hazel had said as she was leaving. Hazel had undoubtedly seen the young child as well, on several occasions. Why was she being so coy about it? Perhaps Hazel recognized ghostly visitations would be a lot to process and would likely take time. Emily would be sure to ask Hazel about it the next time they spoke. There was more to this than her neighbor was letting on, and Emily was eager to discover what it was.

It was nearly two o'clock in the morning, and Emily knew that if she didn't get to her bed in that moment, she'd end up sleeping the whole night on the couch. She nudged Chloe and told her to get up so they could get to bed.

They stumbled into the bedroom, and Emily realized there were still crayons and paper all over the floor that Gina's kids had left. They'd been such troopers all night in her bedroom that she couldn't be too upset about the mess.

Emily bent down to start picking up the construction paper and miscellaneous crayons when one of the drawings caught her attention. It appeared to show a bed, Emily's bed, for the bedspread matched her own bed's "wedding ring" quilt. A little girl hid under the bed. Emily recognized her immediately as Louise, for Gina's daughters had colored her hair jet black — in a Dutch bob style. Was it just a coincidence? There was another figure standing to one side of the room, an older man dressed in overalls. Why would they have drawn that, she wondered. Then, Emily's breath caught in her throat when she saw that they had drawn a third figure, a very tall, thin, blackened humanoid shape with no facial features, just a dark, blank space where a face should have been. This was the very same figure she had seen in the window when she first came to look at the apartment! On that first day seeing the apartment, she had been convinced that her view of the shadowy figure, lurking in the window, was in her imagination, but now she held further evidence, clutched in her sweaty palm. How could these children have imagined this same figure? And Louise? Had they seen them, too?

"Chloe! Can you get in here? You need to see this.

9

Light and shadow

Emily was making the most of her Sunday even though she'd had another restless night, that drawing still on her mind. She'd already done a load of laundry and been to the grocery store to pick up a few items she would need in the week ahead. All her curtains were open. She'd been using the light from a rare sunny day to help chase away her darker thoughts from the night before. She gazed up at the clock on her wall. It was almost 4:30 pm. Anticipating that the evening would come quickly – and bring back the darkness - she proceeded to light a few aromatherapy candles to help her relax while she prepared a fall salad.

    She had hoped to speak with Hazel today. She'd even walked down the hall to knock on her door before she remembered that Hazel had taken an Uber to the airport that morning. Emily recalled her mentioning something about going to visit her eldest son and the grandkids when it dawned on her: Hazel wouldn't be back for another week.

For a moment, she felt anxious and alone. She'd grown accustomed to knowing that Hazel was always just down the hall. With Hazel out of town, she realized she hadn't become particularly friendly with any of her other neighbors in the building. And she'd managed to irritate her neighbor in the apartment directly below her, thanks to Chloe's frequent — and often noisy — visits.

She took her salad to the couch and sat down, tucking a leg under her as she sank into the cushions. She closed her eyes for a moment, inhaled deeply, and drew the bowl closer to her mouth to take a forkful of her delectable feast.

At that moment, her phone began to vibrate on the cushion beside her. She wasn't the kind to leave the sound on, as she never liked the jarring and incessant clatter of any ringtone available to her on her phone. She glanced at the face of the phone. It was Alex.

She'd told herself she'd answer his call if there were ever to be another one, but she was in such an anxious state and was dreading what she anticipated would be an awkward conversation, so she hesitated. It was all she could do to force herself to pick up the phone. She brought the phone to her face and paused for a few more seconds. Then she answered the phone.

"Hi," Emily said, her voice drawn out and lilting, as if she felt the need to apologize for not answering his prior calls.

"Hi," Alex replied, pausing for a moment before he said, "It's really nice to hear your voice, Em."

Emily smiled nervously. "You, too."

"Is this a good time?" asked Alex.

"Yeah, why?"

"I was hoping I'd catch you while you were home... recharging."

"You know me better than anyone."

She was surprised to realize just how much she had missed him. Irrationally, she could feel herself already sliding right back into that warm feeling one has when talking to a best friend or a soul mate; she felt a bit guilty for not hearing him out before she left. It was tempting to simply pick up where they'd left off, as though it were yesterday that they'd last spoken to one another. But they hadn't...and in this moment, Emily regretted that she'd let the time go this long.

"My mom told me you two talked," she said.

"We did. I hope that was alright. I just needed to know you were safe, that you hadn't been kidnapped or something."

"I'm sorry you were worried," Emily answered softly. She saw that it was dark outside, so she took out another match from the side table drawer and lit another candle next to her. She asked Alex, "How has your work been going?" hoping to divert his attention away from her abrupt departure. Alex followed her cue and started telling her about his latest projects.

She thought to herself that this call was going much easier than she'd thought it might. Hearing Alex's voice, it almost didn't even matter to her what they said from here on out. She just wanted to listen to him; she'd always found his voice so soothing and comforting, something she needed right now in this dimly lit room.

As the conversation continued, Emily's anxiousness diminished. Mercifully, Alex wasn't pressing her for an explanation of her leaving NYC, and she was enjoying the conversation as long as they could keep it focused on surface level matters.

The room that had felt a bit foreboding, now seemed warm in the cozy flickering light of the candles. What she felt before this phone call was nothing compared to how she felt now.

"Are they keeping you busy up there in that new job of yours, or do they give you some time off once in a while?" asked Alex.

"I have my weekends, unlike at MSNBC, if that's what you're asking," said Emily, adding, "It's such a nicer pace up here, Babe. You wouldn't believe it."

Emily winced at her careless use of "Babe." Maybe he hadn't noticed. She was worried she was becoming too comfortable too soon before they had really talked about what had happened. She gazed up at the framed print of Louise Brooks, hanging on her wall and thought to herself that Louise would never let such momentary weaknesses show through.

"I can't tell you how wonderful it makes me feel when you call me that," said Alex.

SHIT, she thought.

"Sorry," said Emily. "I didn't mean to say that."

"Please don't...," Alex said, pausing for a moment. "Don't feel weird about it. I want you to feel comfortable with me again."

Emily replied, "I know, but...."

In that moment, something caught Emily's eye. She thought she saw something dark flit by, and she let out a gasp. Her first thought was that a spider had crawled onto something beside one of the candles and that its silhouette was caught briefly by the flickering flame.

"Em, are you okay?" asked Alex.

"Yeah, no... I mean, yeah. I just freaked myself out."

"What happened?"

"Oh, it's nothing," she said, embarrassed that she'd actually made an audible gasp. "The flickering of the candles in here," Emily continued. "I just thought I saw something moving over on the wall, but it was just the way the light was dipping in and out for a sec."

"That's the Em I know, terrified by her own candles," said Alex, chuckling on the other end of the phone.

"I'm not," Emily retorted defensively but froze when she saw a figure standing in the darkened hallway.

"Em? Are you still there?"

"*SHHHHH!*" Emily shot back in a hushed tone.

"Emily, what's happening?"

"I think I just saw somebody," whispered Emily, afraid to move, afraid that whoever was hiding in her apartment might run at her, now that *they* knew *she'd* seen *them*.

Alex continued to try to call out to her, not knowing she had set down her phone. She slowly, carefully raised her arm to the lamp next to her on the couch. She trained her eye on the doorway, trying to acclimate her eyes to the darker part of the room. Someone was there. She could see him. He was a dark mass, and she could now see just a hint of him, peeking out from the hallway leading to her bedroom, but he was there. This was really happening.

Her mind raced. She decided she would grab a vase, flip on the light, then throw the vase and scream as loud as she could to shock the intruder. If nothing else, it might stun him enough for her to run away. She counted down in her mind - *3...2...1.*

She shouted as loudly as she could while immediately turning on the light. The dark mass she had just seen — the definite form of a man peering out from the hallway — was gone. It was as if nothing had even been there a mere second ago, but it had been. She wasn't imagining this!

Still clutching the vase in one hand, Emily quickly grabbed her phone with the other and placed it on speaker mode.

She was shaking. Her racing heart felt as though it was beating out of her chest.

Then she heard Alex.

"Emily! Emily!"

She made her way carefully toward the hallway, the entire area of the room now flooded in light.

"I'm okay," whispered Emily, moving over to the front door.

She opened her front door, reasoning that if anybody was in her apartment, they would have a place to go and wouldn't feel cornered and attack her. She cautiously made her way down the hallway, stopping first to peer into her bedroom. She flipped on the light, and prepared herself for a confrontation, but the room was empty. There were no shadows and no figure. She turned on her phone's flashlight, kneeled down, and hesitantly checked under the bed. Nothing. Next, she checked the closet by flinging open the door, and holding out her phone and the vase in front of her. There was nothing, but she wasn't satisfied until she pushed the clothes back and touched the back wall of the closet, checking to see if there was a portal to some kind of evil Narnia. Then she moved to the bathroom. It was also empty. Shaking and confused, her thoughts returned to the phone, where Alex had been fearing the worst.

"Emily?" Alex whispered.

Emily brought the phone close.

"I'm fine, I'm fine. I'm sorry I scared you," Emily said, closing the front door and locking it again. "I was sure I saw a figure in the hallway, but it must have been a shadow from all the candles." She tried to make light of it, not wanting him to worry. "You know me and candles."

"Em, do you want me to drive up there?" he said, still sounding worried.

"It's okay, really," said Emily, adding, "I have to go into work tomorrow anyway."

"Em, please tell me you'll call me if you need anything."

"I will, really.... I promise, but can you just stay on the phone with me for a while longer?"

"Of course," said Alex.

"Thanks," said Emily as she shuffled back over to the couch and turned on the TV, if only for a little more distraction because she was sure now that she was the only person in the apartment, but she still felt uneasy. *No more candles,* she vowed to herself.

"Will you let me come up there to see you sometime soon?"

Emily paused before giving Alex the answer that she knew he wanted to hear.

"Yes... I will." She could practically feel Alex's relief on the other end of the line.

"Are you still there?" Emily asked, "or did you faint?"

"I'm here. I'm just really happy, but I'm still worried about you."

"I'm fine, really. I'm free next weekend. Do you wanna come up Friday after you get off work?"

"It's a date."

"I'll text you the address," she said. "Bye."

"Okay... goodnight, Em."

Emily hung up and placed the phone back on the couch. She looked around the room, realizing she'd turned on every light in the apartment. And then it dawned on her that she was alone…again.

She picked up her phone and called Chloe.

"Chloe! It's Em, I know it's late notice, but I could really use your company tonight…."

One thing became clear to Emily as she reassessed her living space. This place could no longer provide her with peace and seclusion. For the first time since moving into this apartment, Emily was fully convinced she wasn't alone.

10

The Realization

In the morning after very little sleep, Chloe and Emily were having breakfast, when Chloe, having enough of the tense silence, burst out "I would rather not be that chick who dies stupidly in a horror movie by not doing anything, aka hiding behind the swinging curtains of chainsaws - I mean shadows - in the corridor! Dude, seriously!"

"I'm sure I was just overwhelmed. Talking to Alex was a bit stressful." Emily said defensively. "I'm sure I was just overreacting. I don't want to blow this out of proportion. Maybe I should see someone for some relaxation techniques? There's this meditation podcast I've been thinking about trying."

Waving her hands dramatically, Chloe spit out, "Podcast?! That's your solution to this? What the fuck?! I thought maybe you were just stressed, but those creepy, fucked up drawings convinced me that we at least need to consider a paranormal cause. It would be one thing if those kids were just into drawing messed up figures under the bed, but they drew *your* messed up stuff. There are three options: we get out of here; we buy a pickup truck just to fill the back with a fuck-ton of sage; or we get a medium in here to unfuck the aura or remove whatever is in this place!" Rolling her eyes, and then imitating Emily in a tiny girlish voice, Chloe mocked her friend once more, "a podcast will solve *all* my problems - no nothing to see here, everything is super-duper fine."

"Geeze, maybe you should listen to a calming podcast or two," Emily muttered.

"I'm not the one with the super haunted apartment!" Chloe exclaimed. "I'm a little worried you aren't as freaked out as I am." She continued, still trying to convince Emily, "It's all fun and games before heads start spinning around, spewing pea soup with wild abandon."

"Okay. Fine. I get it. How about we call a medium? The one from our Halloween segment?" Emily grudgingly suggested.

The medium she referred to was featured in a Halloween tv segment a few weeks earlier. The network wanted to do a bit on a local, reportedly haunted location – Rolling Hills Asylum, in East Bethany, New York. It was a popular tourist destination during the month of October for "getting one's spook on." Part of the segment would include a medium – one who can communicate with the "other side" – who would comment on the "paranormal activity" in the area to help the small, local holiday-themed businesses. As was the standard for any feature, they had contacted several of the medium's clients without her knowledge, to ensure that the medium was credible and charismatic enough for an on-camera interview. No one they spoke with while preparing the piece suspected that this woman was a fraud; in fact, she came with excellent recommendations, including reports that she often worked with local police to solve missing persons cases. Having watched enough psychics on TV in the past, Emily was aware that at least some of what they said should be taken with a grain of salt. It had been her experience that many of them simply had a talent for picking up on minute cues in the feedback they got from the people they were reading. This medium, Madeleine Bloom, however, seemed, to Emily, an entirely unique and seemingly trustworthy character.

Chloe still had Madeleine's card and called her immediately. Madeleine was happy to come right over, eschewing her other business for the day, as she felt grateful for their tv promotion. She was pleased to be able to return the favor and potentially make more business contacts.

While waiting for the aforementioned medium, Emily forced Chloe to listen to a calming podcast.

PANDORA'S BOX

11

The Boogeyman

Chloe, in her initial phone call to the psychic medium, had mentioned that Emily believed her apartment was haunted; Emily and Chloe decided that neither of them should bring up Emily's encounter with the shadow figure. By not giving her any details, they avoided influencing the woman's "reading."

* * *

"Hi, Mrs. Bloom. It's great to see you again," said Emily, extending her hand to the woman as she entered Emily's apartment. "Thank you for agreeing to come on such short notice."

The woman appeared to be in her mid-fifties and was heavy-set and a little taller than Emily remembered. She had clearly dyed, red hair and wore a charcoal turtleneck sweater and finely creased slacks. With a charming grin, Madeleine returned Emily's greetings and shook her hand.

"*You're* an interesting one," Madeleine quipped mysteriously, peering into Emily's eyes.

"Oh?"

"This has been a long time coming hasn't it, honey?" Madeleine asked.

Emily hesitated. "What do you mean?" she asked. For a moment, the false tone in her voice kept her from meeting the woman's gaze.

"It's alright," said Madeleine. "You don't have to tell me about it if it makes you uncomfortable."

A puzzled expression appeared on Chloe's face, and Emily returned the gaze with a tiny shrug of her shoulders, preferring to keep some things private even from Chloe.

The woman closed her eyes and took a long, deep breath. Slowly strolling around the living room, she paused and looked down the hall.

"I'm being drawn down the hallway," said Madeleine. She turned to Emily and asked with some formality, "May I?"

Emily nodded, and she and Chloe followed the woman down the hallway into Emily's bedroom.

"What a bright and welcoming space you've made of this room, my dear," said Madeleine. Then she added, "You do know she died in this room, don't you?"

Emily looked at Chloe, her eyes widening.

"I'm not picking up a name just yet," the woman continued quietly. Realizing she should convey more, she added, "Oh, I'm sorry.... It didn't occur recently or anything."

The information did little to put Emily at ease.

Madeleine looked about the room; pushing up her sleeves, she raised her arms taking in the atmosphere, "Whoever she is, she's still very active…and she's a spitfire!" She stopped briefly before continuing, "*Wow*, she was a pretty one." Madeleine turned her attention back to Emily. "You've seen her before, haven't you?" she asked. "She probably appeared to you as a flesh-and-blood person, though, completely solid. Not in a spirit form, yes?"

Emily nodded.

Madeleine returned to the main room and addressed Emily once again.

"How old did she look to you when you saw her?"

"Maybe eight or nine," Emily answered.

"She can present herself as she would have appeared at any point throughout her life. She might appear as a child to another child, or she might choose to appear as a thirty-year-old to an adult. I'm a little surprised she appeared to you as a child."

Chloe asked, "How old is she…presenting herself to you, Madeleine?"

"Oh, I'd guess she's around nineteen or twenty. She's a real beauty. I'd have to guess she's from the 1920s. A flapper type. But this one would've stood out in a crowd."

Madeleine turned and noticed the framed print of Louise. Raising a trembling hand, she pointed, "Wait, that's her!"

"Yes," Emily said. "Her name is Louise." Then she asked, "Does the way she's presenting herself to *you* have any significance?"

"Typically, it implies she never thought of herself as an old person," the woman observed. "I think she felt very frustrated in her later years. To anyone who met her then, she just looked like an old woman, but in her mind, she was nineteen. Imagine how that must have felt. She was a youthful, lively young thing trapped in a shell of a body by the time she passed."

Madeleine clutched her chest, wincing in pain as she began to speak. "She's showing me she had an issue with her lungs," Madeleine rasped, refocusing her attention back to the spirit. "Okay, back off…back off. I felt it."

Madeleine looked back at Emily and Chloe, a pained expression on her face as she fanned herself with her hands. "I'm guessing she was a smoker."

The woman took another pause and closed her eyes. Emily and Chloe stood silently watching as Madeleine continued, "She's telling me that she tried to warn you about another presence."

"No, that never happened," Emily said, shaking her head as she sat down on the couch, Chloe joining her quickly. "I remember it distinctly…. She told me I don't belong here. She called me 'pretty' but told me I'd better keep my mouth shut or I'd find myself 'dead in the basement.'"

A feeling of dread grew in Emily. She wondered if the figure she'd seen the previous evening was tied to the threat.

"Madeleine, can you please try to talk to this spirit again?" asked Chloe, attempting to comfort her friend. "Can you find out why she said what she did?"

Madeleine closed her eyes once more and began to walk around the room, pressing her fingers against her temples.

"Okay, okay, I think it's becoming clearer in my mind, now, what must have happened," said Madeleine, stopping in the middle of the room.

She moved to the couch and sat down next to Emily and began to speak again in a soft, reassuring tone. "This stuff, spirit world stuff," she said, "it's kind of hit or miss. You see, they're not always able to convey a completely coherent thought or message."

Emily turned to look at Madeleine, having calmed a little; she listened to the medium explain.

"It takes an extreme amount of energy to manifest, you know, to appear in solid form, and they don't always get it right."

Madeleine closed her eyes again, as if listening to someone who was talking to her from the other side.

"She didn't know another way to tell you, so she simply spit back at you what someone had once told her. Given the way she appeared to you, this all must have happened to her when she was just a child. That may be why she appeared to you as a little girl."

"So, are you saying that she was telling me what somebody said to *her*?" asked Emily.

"That's my hunch, dear. At some point in that little girl's life, somebody may have said those awful things to her." Madeleine extended her arm and rubbed Emily's back in a gesture of comfort. "I think there's at least one other distinct energy; it's possible that there are more that I'm feeling in this apartment, but there's so much going on in here, at the moment, that it's difficult to separate everything and make sense of it all," Madeleine said, looking up and tracing the walls with her eyes. "Whoever said those things to that girl, I think he makes himself known in this space, too…. He must have followed her somehow… but all I keep getting is the image of a non-descript person in overalls." Madeleine paused for a moment, her eyes closed tightly. "Wait! I'm picking up on something else now. I've never seen anything quite like this one before. It's here in the room with us now."

Emily and Chloe exchanged nervous glances.

"You said… *'it's* here?' What do you mean… it?" Emily asked tremulously.

Madeleine continued gingerly, "I'm hesitant to say since I'm not sure how you'll react."

"Please, just tell me," Emily said.

The woman's gaze traveled slowly up the wall, and she pointed with her outstretched arm.

"It's almost insect-like…and it's crawling up the wall," Madeleine said, pointing at the ceiling.

"How is that possible?" Emily asked, feeling increasingly alarmed.

"The one in the overalls. This one's been here for a long time," said Madeleine, ignoring Emily's question for the moment to glance around the room once more.

"But what about this other thing, this insect-looking thing?" insisted Emily.

Madeleine refocused her attention back to Emily. "If that thing was once a living, breathing person, it's apparently figured out how to change its appearance into completely nonhuman forms. I've never really seen anything quite like it before."

"But why would it appear to you in such a disturbing way?" asked Emily.

"I'm guessing he may not have been a particularly powerful sort when he was alive. Now that he's on the other side, he obviously takes great pleasure in presenting himself that way to torment both the living — and the dead — to maximum affect."

The medium glared at the wall, then looked over at the pair before continuing, "he must be a real predator. You catch my meaning?"

Emily nodded, crossing her arms, and pressing herself into

the couch. Chloe's leg started to bounce, exuding nervous energy.

"I thought you might," Madeleine said, nodding compassionately and taking hold of Emily's arm.

Madeleine scooted herself forward on the couch, collecting her thoughts.

"This entity, here in the room with us right now, has been in a sort of hibernation... until recently," she said, confused, turning her attention to Emily once more. "If I had to guess, I'd say that a lot of the energy I'm picking up in this space — the feminine presence, the form I saw wearing the overalls, and this particular nasty-looking one in the room with us now — they're drawn to *you* somehow."

"What do I do about all of this?" Emily asked. "Is there something you can do to make all of it just go away?"

"Yeah," Chloe blurted. "How do we get out of this fu... freaking creep show?"

The medium laid her hand on Emily's hand.

"All I can do is reassure you both that they can't hurt you if you don't give them any power over you."

"And that insect, spider-looking thing..." Chloe jabbed, "What about him?"

"In life, that entity was probably a nobody. He was weak, so he more than likely resorted to taking advantage of others who couldn't defend themselves."

Emily bowed her head, taking in all that Madeleine was saying to her.

"What do you suggest I do?" asked Emily. "This is my home."

"These types of men, whether in life or after they've transitioned over, they're on the lookout for any sign of vulnerability in others," said Madeleine. "Don't show them any. Like you said, dear, this *is* your home. So, tell them so! Make it clear to them that they're not welcome here."

Emily slumped forward and clutched her temples, tears spilling down her cheeks. Chloe placed her hand on Emily's back.

Chloe anxiously whispered to the medium, "How is she supposed to 'not show any vulnerability' when a predator spidery ghost shows up? Like what the actual fuck? Are you serious right now?"

The medium rose and motioned for Chloe and Emily to approach.

"Can we speak downstairs or outside?" Madeleine asked in a hushed tone.

Emily and Chloe exchanged nods and gathered their jackets before exiting the apartment. Emily locked the door behind them.

"What's going on?" Emily asked as they made their way to the elevator.

"That negative entity appears to be trapped in your space," the woman explained in a whisper. "For whatever reason, it's unable to escape. It would seem that… for now, at least, the little girl appears to be the only one of them that's able to travel freely throughout the building."

They stood by the elevator doors, waiting for the elevator to return to the third-floor landing.

"I'd prefer to speak with you quietly outside," whispered Madeleine. "It'll be more secure that way."

Emily nodded, and the three of them rode the elevator down to the lobby, where they exited the elevator and walked out the front door into the cold, crisp night air.

Madeleine shifted her gaze to address both Emily and Chloe.

"Is there some sort of crawl space in this building?"

"I have no idea." Emily stated. "Why do you ask?"

Chloe furrowed her brow, not understanding where the medium was going with this.

"I'm picking up an image of a little crawl space. I'm sensing it's significant in some way."

"Significant to the little girl ghost?" Emily asked.

"I'm not certain," the woman said. "What I'm picking up from her is that wherever this location is, it's not in your apartment. She apparently doesn't want those other spirits knowing about it."

The woman took Emily's hands in hers, her tone even more serious. "It just hit me, dear..., *this* is about you! Something about you — either now, or maybe something from your past. It's not clear to me yet."

"What do you mean, it's about me?"

Madeleine leaned in closer to Emily. "There was so much emotional energy hitting me up there in your apartment, it was hard to discern what was what. Now that we're out of that space, I'm able to focus a little more, but I'm afraid you're not going to like what I'm about to say."

"Please, just tell me, whatever it is." Emily pressed Madeleine, emphatically.

"That thing I saw crawling up the wall in your apartment..." Madeleine lowered her voice to Emily and paused for a moment, before continuing once more, "It's attached to you!"

"What does that mean?" Emily pleaded. "How is that even possible?"

Chloe interjected sarcastically, "Super. Fucking. Helpful. How is she supposed to figure this out? And once again, how do we not show 'vulnerability' to that spidery thing. How are we even supposed to go back in there, like ever? Emily, please, please, please, come stay at my place. I'll help you get out of your lease."

"Chloe, please!" Emily shouted, trying to focus on what Madeleine had just told her. "Are you saying that it's somehow taken an interest in me? Is it like attached to me whenever I'm up there?"

Madeleine just stood there, motionless, staring back at Emily, as if she didn't want to say any more than she'd already said.

"Wait," blurted Emily, "are you suggesting that it came here… with me?"

"I don't know. When I saw it as an insect-like creature, that is how it was projecting its appearance to me. That's not what it is, and anyone who isn't psychic, might only see it as a fleeting shadow, harmless at this stage. When I say that something is attached, I mean that you have a connection to it that you are currently unaware of, but that isn't the main problem with the apartment right now. The dominant entity in the apartment will leave if you are strong and establish that space as belonging to you. If you are still having problems, I will come back, but that is really what works for most of these types of situations. Above all, don't worry; I'll be here for you throughout the process."

12

And Pretty Maids All in a Row

"Hey, Mary!" called a neighbor girl as she raced to catch up with her on the way to school. "Did you take the popcorn yesterday?"

Mary shook her head and smiled back. She could see that her friend had fetched the prize this day.

"He put it right there on the edge of his porch, all tied up with a ribbon and everything," said her friend, gushing with glee.

With a few pieces of popcorn in her palm, the girl extended her arm to Mary, who was another of the select, privileged few who'd been fortunate enough to have caught the favor of the neighborhood handyman.

Mary plucked the treat from her friend's hand and popped it into her mouth. A few small fragments fell down the front of her dress.

As they strolled along, mainly in silence, she was reminded of how wonderful it had been to go by the old man's house and see that he'd left a gift for her to fetch. Usually, she'd tiptoe up to the edge of the porch, take the treasure, and flee. The other girls did the same, and each hoped to arrive early enough to snatch the treat before another little girl scooped it up.

She thought on it some more and determined that she would walk by that porch tomorrow before any of the others had a chance to claim the prize.

The following morning, Mary made a point of getting up and out of the house before any of her siblings.

The air was slightly brisk, and the sun had not yet risen over the rooflines. The home of Mr. Flowers – at least that was what everyone called him - was not too far ahead. She scanned the area, checking to see whether anybody else was nearby. She would be the early bird today.

As she approached the home, she noticed another modest but full cloth sack on the porch. It had the same ribbon as the others. Mary looked forward to bragging about the treat in class when the teachers weren't around.

She approached the front of the house with caution and deliberation, then bent over to fetch her present. She grinned as she held it up to her nose. It was popcorn once more, one of her favorites, second only to chocolate.

She caught a glimpse of something out of the corner of her eye. She could see through the curtain that someone was peering out of the front window. It had to be Mr. Flowers. She was feeling mischievous on this particular day, so she stepped up on the porch and walked to the screen door. Normally, she'd be concerned about disturbing him, but she could see that he'd already seen her.

Having been seen taking the treat, she decided she would ask Mr. Flowers if the treat was meant for her. She raised her small hand and began knocking....

13

A Secret

Madeleine Bloom had given Emily a lot to consider. Madeleine had even called attention to a crawl space. That piqued Emily's interest. It gave her total confidence that Madeleine had truly picked up on several other strange things she couldn't have known any other way.

The reference to a crawl space was extremely personal, something that had tormented Emily for the better part of her life. It was something so intimate, so private, that she hadn't spoken of it to anyone — not her parents, nor even Alex — but now Emily felt compelled to try to understand why the medium focused on that one, specific vision. The psychic would have had no idea of its significance, but the fact that she would divine that — out of thin air — convinced Emily that she needed to treat the infestation that Madeleine warned her about seriously. And she began to fear how her own experiences may be playing a part in her current, chilling predicament.

Sitting alone in her apartment, Emily gazed up at the framed print of Louise; she now realized that she needed to find out more about her. It might give her some more insight into what was plaguing her home and how to stop it, besides "not showing vulnerability."

14

With Silver Bells and Cockleshells

She clutched the intricate silver chain tightly and raised her arm, allowing the locket to dangle in front of her face. She'd noticed it on her mother's nightstand and "borrowed" it even though she was forbidden from touching it. She knew better than to take the locket from her parents' room, but she decided that it couldn't hurt to play with it a little. Now, back in her own bedroom, she was mesmerized by the way light reflected off the locket, casting brief streaks of light along her wall.

She placed the locket back into her palm and pressed one of her nails into the side, releasing the latch that had been holding it shut. She pried it open like one would a clamshell, revealing the photographs inside: her father on the left and her lovely mother on the right.

She snapped the locket shut and slipped the necklace over her head, carefully lowering it around her neck and allowing the locket to fall and hang just above her stomach.

She had barely put it on to check the fit in the mirror when she heard footsteps coming down the hallway. They were measured, loud steps; she knew instantly that her father was approaching.

She yanked the necklace from her neck and dashed over to her bed, where a small cigar box lay. It was constructed of wood and featured inlaid accent strips that formed a frame along the top lid's edge. Inside was a collection of trinkets she'd gathered. A bejeweled cat brooch, some loose pennies discovered on one of her many walks, and a piece of linen cloth in the shape of a pouch with a pink ribbon tied in a bow that held together what was essentially a handful of polished rocks. The latter was a gift from the man she'd spoken with on the porch weeks before, who'd given her the candy. He'd been doting on her for some time.

As soon as she heard the footsteps come to a halt outside her door, she threw the necklace into the box, slammed the lid shut, and slid the box beneath her bed.

She had just hopped onto the bed when the doorknob began to turn.

Her father leaned in, and she could smell the cherry tobacco burning in the pipe he held in the other hand.

"It's bedtime, Princess," he said sternly.

"Yes, Papa."

"Sleep tight," he whispered as he closed the door.

"Goodnight, Papa."

15

Louise

Emily became fascinated with Louise. In her spare time, she began reading *Lulu in Hollywood*; in her autobiography, Louise Brooks recounted her early life, including the fact that she lived with her family in Cherryvale, Kansas. Emily was astounded to find out that she was from the same small town as Louise Brooks! After Cherryvale, Louise went off to pursue her dancing and film career in New York and Hollywood. Emily was captivated by Louise, who had died nearly a decade before Emily was born. These were not the banal memories of an aging Hollywood has-been. These were vivid experiences recounted in the voice of a young, vivacious woman. Despite the passage of many years, Emily felt as though Louise was speaking directly to her as her contemporary.

Her influence was everywhere. Liza Minnelli's portrayal of Sally Bowles in *Cabaret* was inspired by Louise. Cyd Charisse personified her in the "Broadway Melody" dance number in

Singin' in the Rain. In the film *Something Wild*, the character played by Melanie Griffith, in a jet-black bob, dubs herself "Lulu" after Brooks's character in *Pandora's Box.*

It became less surprising, Emily reflected after delving deeper into Louise's life, that she had piqued the interest of so many who met her. She was young and attractive, and her overwhelming sensuality made her an object of desire, which led to a proclivity for dalliance after dalliance. At 15, Louise was invited to New York to perform with the renowned Denishawn School of Dancing and Related Arts. Within weeks, she was ejected from two hotels because of her scandalous conduct, which included dancing on the rooftop in sheer sleepwear. Louise's temperament and entitled attitude soon became too much for the dance academy founders to tolerate, and she was dismissed. After moving in with a friend, she found work, almost immediately, dancing with the Ziegfield follies, which she did for the next several years, despite being a minor. Then, at the age of 19, she signed a deal with Paramount and began her silent film career.

Emily felt a connection to Louise in a way she never imagined possible. They were both raised in the same town in Kansas, and both were drawn eventually to New York – and both ended up in Rochester, which was eerie. Louise also embodied qualities Emily envied. Louise possessed an abundance of natural ability in an impressive range of roles: dancer, actor, writer, and painter. Above all, Emily wished for Louise's confidence, especially with men.

Emily was proud of her recent move to Rochester. It was an uncharacteristically bold move for her. Too much of her life, though, was marked by a fear of taking risks. However, Emily disliked carrying this burden, this fear. Emily had spent nearly two decades going through life as if she were wearing a burlap sack. Gradually, Emily came to despise the fact that Alex was the only man whom she had allowed to get close to her whereas Louise seemed to effortlessly date and enjoy men without second guessing or worrying about consequences. Emily always worried about the consequences. She craved spontaneity and a sense of carefree confidence. Louise, on the other hand, wanted to be seen more seriously as an artist, so much so that she left Hollywood fame behind because she felt that she didn't have enough respect. She broke her deal with Paramount and decided to go to Europe to shoot a film in Germany with a director of some renown.

Emily was disappointed to find that she did share a few less positive characteristics with Louise. Both women had a mercurial temper and a burning desire to reinvent themselves. Louise directed these characteristics outward while Emily tended to focus these characteristics inward. In addition, Emily learned that both Louise and she had similarly negative views of themselves.

In her later years, Louise wrote to one of her brothers, Theo:
"I have been taking stock of my 50 years since I left Wichita in 1922 at the age of 15 to become a dancer with Ruth St. Denis and Ted Shawn. How I have existed fills me with horror. For I have failed in everything — spelling, arithmetic, riding, tennis, golf; dancing, singing, acting; wife, mistress, whore, friend. Even cooking. And I do not excuse myself with the usual escape of 'not trying.' I tried with all my heart."[1]

---

[1] Paris, Barry. *Louise Brooks*. Alfred A. Knopf, 1987, P. 550.

As Emily read the letter, she couldn't help but marvel at how someone whose life inspired so many could feel like such a failure. Their lives seemed so different, but Emily could still understand just how Louise felt.

Given Hazel's relationship with Louise toward the end of her life, Emily wondered whether Hazel had greater insight into Louise's psyche than Emily had discovered during her research. She'd been eager to speak to Hazel about their shared interaction with Louise's ghost. Hazel didn't appear to be upset by her own paranormal encounters. So, why, Emily wondered, was she herself singled out in such a disturbing way?

One evening after work, Emily crossed the hall and knocked gently on Hazel's door. The TV inside Hazel's apartment was turned up very loud, but Emily could hear Hazel's slippered feet shuffling across the floor to the door.

"Who is it?" Hazel said through the door in a singsong fashion.

"It's just me, Hazel. It's Emily."

"Oh, what a pleasant surprise, dear," Hazel said as she opened the door. "I've been thinking about coming over to see you."

"Oh? Why is that?"

"Well, I wanted to catch up and see how you're doing."

Hazel took Emily's hand and pulled her to the couch.

Emily said, "I came by to ask you about Louise. I've been doing a lot of reading about her; I've found her life to be so fascinating."

"Oh, she was a firecracker when she was in her prime, that's for sure," said Hazel. Then she added with a grin, "I didn't know her back when she was a young thing, of course. By the time I met her, I wasn't much older than 40, and Louise was in her early 70's."

"What do you mean?"

"I just mean to say that I met her at the tail end, when I was not much older than you are now, and she was the age I am now."

"I think I understand where you're coming from," Emily said. "From what I've read about her, she seemed pretty cantankerous in her later years, unlike you of course."

"She could be...at times," said Hazel. "She wasn't necessarily a jar of honey to me when we first met. It took her time to trust me. To tell you the truth, I think she was intrigued by a book I was reading at the time, a biography on Charlie Chaplin. She saw me reading it in the laundry room while I was waiting for my clothes to dry. We started talking a bit about the book, and then she told me that she knew Charlie, and that the biography got it all wrong. We started to spend more time together, but she was always stubborn about my helping her with her groceries, etc., when she became frail.

Hazel looked down for a moment, as if considering her next words more carefully.

"She really was a wonderfully sweet person, don't get me wrong," said Hazel. "But she could be ornery...and for good reason. God knows she had every Tom, Dick, and Harry wanting her time, her attention, her memories. By the 1980s, she'd stopped allowing visitors to come up and see her — you know, film historians, critics, and the like. She said it had just gotten too difficult to perform for them."

"Why did she feel the need to entertain them?" asked Emily.

"She told me she needed to be 'on' in front of strangers who she believed would delight in any mistakes she might make in order to profit from articles about an aging 'has been.' I think she preferred that everyone remember her as she was in her film days. Even she preferred to keep that youthful image of herself in her own mind. She told me how, in her fifties, she would sit for hours and watch her old movies at 'Eastman House.'"

"What's that?" Emily interjected.

Hazel continued, "It's actually called the George Eastman Museum, Dear; it's a photography museum and one of the oldest film archives in the country. George Eastman invented Kodak film. His home, here in Rochester, later became the museum. And it was the museum's curator James Card that had become yet another admirer of Louise. Seeing that she was not doing well in New York – her alcoholism was taking a toll – he convinced her to move to Rochester to be away from some of her bad habits and so that she could review her old films as part of her research for her autobiography. In my late thirties, or thereabouts, I also worked at the museum; I worked in the giftshop, but that was well after Louise had stopped going there altogether. By the time I met her, her emphysema and arthritis had become too much for her to get out at all anymore. She had long since abandoned her work on her autobiography."

Hazel paused for a moment before continuing. "She'd mostly confined herself to letter writing when she was feeling well enough. She'd type most letters and then sign the bottom, but even *that* became too difficult in the last few years due to the arthritis."

Emily was heartbroken. It was difficult to hear Hazel describe someone so different from the spirited, confident young woman Emily had met in Louise's early writings. She wondered what had happened to turn her into a reclusive, and less than friendly, older woman.

"I would usually come by in the evenings and make sure she'd eaten something, and if she hadn't, I'd make something for her to eat. I'd do the same for her in the mornings, too. I just wanted to make sure she was okay. Sometimes, she'd have good days, and we would talk about all sorts of things. She was so incredibly bright. But sometimes, I'd open the door, and the first thing she did was ask me if I'd brought a gun. It became her little joke between us."

Hazel's tone quieted a bit. She pulled a tissue from her pocket and wiped her nose.

"I remember the last evening we talked on the phone," Hazel continued. "She asked me if I'd remember her when she was gone. I said, 'Of course, Louise. I'll remember you for as long as I live, and after that, just a little more....'"

Hazel smiled sadly. Emily placed her hand on Hazel's shoulder to comfort her. And then Emily's curiosity took over. "Did Louise ever talk to you about why she made such impetuous decisions throughout her life?"

Hazel scooted herself off the couch and shuffled to her kitchen.

"Can I get you anything, dear?"

"No, I'm fine. Thank you, though."

Hazel turned and addressed Emily more directly.

"Did I ever talk to you about Mr. Flowers?"

Emily shook her head.

Hazel poured herself a cup of coffee and made her way back over to the couch.

"Louise spoke of him only once to me," began Hazel. "She'd had her whole life to put it into perspective by that point, but I could see it still bothered her a lot. And when she told me what had happened, I completely understood."

Emily was intrigued. She'd come across nothing regarding this person in any of her previous research.

"Mr. Flowers was a local handyman who did odd jobs for some of the wealthier women in town. The Stricklers, down the street, hired him quite often. Louise told me that the Stricklers had this beautiful Victorian home. She spent a great deal of time over there. It became sort of a second home to her. She was just a little thing then, no more than eight or nine. But she loved spending time over there because Mrs. Strickler — 'Tot,' she was called — had a house that was full of music and wall-to-wall books."

Hazel scooted closer to Emily as if she was revealing the latest gossip.

"Tot was a lot like Louise's mother, Myra, in her love of music," Hazel continued. "But they were different in one very important and distinct way. Myra was not a nurturer — at all. She pretty much let the kids have the run of the house, for better or worse. She really couldn't be bothered most of the time, and she treated her own children as if they were an afterthought. If she showed interest in any of them, it was in Louise — specifically her talent for dancing. These days, you'd probably call someone like that a bit of a stage mother. Aside from Louise's gift for dance, Myra wanted nothing else to do with raising her. That's where Mrs. Strickler came in."

Hazel sipped from her cup and cleared her throat. "Mrs. Strickler was the mother Louise never had," she said. "That's why Louise loved spending time over there. She got all the attention from Tot that her own mother never gave her."

She paused and placed her cup on the table beside them. "It was during these visits that Mr. Flowers, who had been doing a lot of work inside the Stricklers' house, had an opportunity to see a lot of Louise. To everyone, he seemed a kindly man, but he showed an awful lot of attention to the little girls in the neighborhood. It had gotten to the point that he'd been leaving treats and candy for them on his porch on a regular basis...."

Emily was all too aware of where this story was leading. However, she sat silently — and uncomfortably — while Hazel recounted the rest of the story.

"One day, Louise saw that he'd left another treat on his porch. Most of the little girls would just snatch the treat and run off, but Louise was feeling particularly brave this one day and made the mistake of knocking on his door."

Hazel became silent, and her expression grew more serious.

"He invited her into his house and then took her innocence."

Emily took in a breath as Hazel continued. "She was only nine years old. Can you imagine? It's truly heartbreaking. That sort of thing wasn't even talked about back then. And it was pretty clear that Louise's mother didn't understand how to deal with it, either. When Louise finally got the courage to tell her what had happened to her, Myra blamed Louise, saying she led him on."

Emily remained still as Hazel handed her the last piece of the puzzle she was looking for.

"Poor thing," Hazel said. "She told me that every bad decision she ever made she could trace back to that terrible man."

Emily had tears in her eyes.

Hazel offered her a tissue, thinking that Emily's tears were for Louise, but, in reality, Emily had just discovered that she and Louise shared yet one more aspect of their lives than she'd previously understood.

Wiping her eyes, Emily thought of her nightmares. Every

few weeks since she had moved into the apartment, she would awaken from a nightmare in the middle of the night, unable to recall the specifics of the dream, but disturbed by the vision she had just had. The dark, hollow feeling she felt now after hearing Hazel's story reminded her of how she felt after the most recent nightmare. Though she didn't reveal it to Hazel, it felt as though Louise had been attempting to show her all the things that Hazel had just explained, as though the two were bound by something more than just an apartment. She promised herself that she would think about it further on her own.

16

Alex

It was the first weekend of December, and Emily was both thrilled and nervous. She'd been communicating with Alex more often over the last several weeks. For weeks, he had been intending to visit for a weekend, but because of changes in his work schedule and the Thanksgiving holiday – with its inherent family duties – this was their first chance to spend time together. Emily had decorated her apartment but still wanted a Christmas tree. She felt that a trip together with Alex to get a tree would be an excellent way for the two of them to avoid the possible awkwardness of spending time together after months apart.

Emily's favorite time of year was Christmas. It was a season when she didn't need an excuse to stay inside and bundle up. And she adored the hues that accompanied the season — mostly seen in the beautiful lights and lovely vintage decorations she'd collected over the years and placed with great delight around her apartment.

Alex also loved the season. Emily had conditioned him when they started dating to follow whatever holiday traditions she proposed. Alex was unconcerned. His family had few traditions of their own, and he was more than willing to embrace Emily's. He enjoyed them and the way Emily lit up during the season.

Earlier in the evening, Alex had called while Emily was still at work to let her know that he would arrive at her place within the hour. Sometime later, after Emily arrived home, she parked in the garage beneath the building and was making her way up the ramp from the garage when she saw Alex drive up in a rental car. She waved to him and motioned for him to drive down the ramp into the garage.

Alex urged Emily to join him for the remainder of the ride. She jumped into the passenger side and slammed the door shut. The warmth of Alex's vehicle engulfed Emily as she sat rubbing her hands together and breathing into them for yet more warmth. She directed Alex to a guest parking space next to her car. He turned off the ignition and leaned across the vehicle to Emily's side, kissing her cheek.

He smiled and said, "I've missed you."

Emily returned the grin, searching for anything to say in order to keep the conversation light.

"Shall we grab your things and bring 'em up?" she asked, unable to hide her blush.

They exited the vehicle, and Alex retrieved his travel bag from the trunk.

"You show the way," Alex replied, closing the trunk.

They passed through the laundry room and into the ground-level corridor. When they reached the lobby, Emily pressed the elevator's button to open the doors and take them to the third floor. They both entered the tiny elevator and stood side by side, watching the floor numbers change. For once, Emily was grateful for how cramped the elevator could be. She threw her arms around Alex and whispered into his ear, "I've missed you, too."

Once settled into the apartment, Emily and Alex prepared dinner together. It was the perfect activity to help them both feel comfortable with each other again.

The evening was going as Emily had hoped. They'd had a nice candle-lit dinner and comfortably made small talk while they ate. Emily opened a second bottle of wine. She poured wine into each of their glasses, glancing at Alex briefly to try to gauge his mood. He'd grown quiet, and she could feel herself becoming a little anxious.

"Look, I'm really sorry," Emily said, then paused to collect her full thought. "I'm sorry for the way I handled things back in Chelsea. I should have talked to you."

"I'm trying to understand your perspective." Alex said in a soft tone. "I've had a lot of time to think about all of it, and, I probably was giving off a totally guilty vibe… for weeks…."

"A month," Emily interjected, nervously. "Well, two months, if I'm being totally honest."

"Look, Emily, you have to know that I'm your biggest fan," Alex said.

Emily nodded. She knew he was telling her the truth.

"I would never do anything intentionally to hurt you…ever," he said.

"I know."

"Cheating?" Alex asked. "Me? You know me better than anyone, Em. Why would I ever cheat? You're the best thing that ever happened to me!"

Emily smiled sheepishly. It made her feel wonderful to hear Alex say such things.

"It's just that when you started working so late all the time, I started to work late to keep my mind distracted" Emily said. "But I still let my imagination run wild. And then, when you *were* home, you acted weird and uncomfortable when you were around me."

Alex lowered his head. He looked slightly embarrassed.

"I should have just told you…from the beginning," Alex said.

"Told me what?"

"Look, I was working late over those months; I was summarizing some high-profile cases and preparing reports on each of them for one of the partners at the firm; I'd been taking on extra work in order to impress them enough that they might give me a bonus. My boss knew I wanted to make some extra money, and she hinted that I was in line for something big!"

Emily waited in silence.

"Em, I got it! I got the bonus, and it was way more than I expected."

Emily gave him a puzzled look. She was baffled as to how money was even a factor in this. It was never the focus of their relationship, and she never put any pressure on him to provide for the two of them financially.

"I've been putting in all the extra hours," Alex said finally, "because I wanted to propose to you!"

Emily was stunned. Her mind began reeling as she realized just how badly she'd interpreted the last several months.

"I wasn't about to propose without a ring," Alex said. "And I wanted to get that bonus in order to afford the ring and set aside something for wedding preparations or at least get us started saving toward our honeymoon."

Emily was deeply embarrassed. She really had screwed things up, almost to the point that she might have lost Alex forever.

"I mean, admittedly, given the way you were acting toward me whenever I *was* home," Alex explained, "giving you more space — putting in the extra time at work — seemed the best course of action."

Alex moved closer to Emily, then took her hand.

"Em, seriously…you bring out the best in me. You're the only girl I would ever work that hard for," he said with a wink. "I know now that I probably should communicate better."

Alex sat back into his chair and took a sip of his wine.

"I was blind-sided when I came home from work to find that you'd left," Alex said. "I had no idea what was going on. When I couldn't reach you, seriously Em, I thought you might have been kidnapped or something. I was about to open a missing persons file when I thought to call your mom. She initially explained to me that you were safe, but she eventually told me that you were staying with Chloe, here in Rochester. I knew that you were upset with me for some reason, but, since I now knew you were safe, I figured I could just wait until we had an opportunity to finally talk things through."

Emily slowly swirled her wine, ashamed to meet Alex's eyes.

"I'm so glad you're here now," Emily said. "I'm so glad we're finally able to talk about this."

"Look, Em, I completely understand now that I only made the misunderstanding worse by not telling you why I was working so late, and I apologize for that. We'd talked a little bit about marriage before…. I don't know why I felt this need to go sneaking around to make this grand gesture. I just wanted my proposal to be everything you may have dreamed of in your life, but now I realize I should have talked to you about it."

Emily grabbed Alex's hand and held it tightly.

"Let's figure our way forward, and we can start by agreeing to always be honest with each other in the future. I should have also talked to you about my insecurities. I'm sorry for jumping to conclusions. I should have trusted that you had my best interests at heart."

* * *

After dinner, as they sat on the couch, Emily began showing Alex a side of herself he hadn't seen before, at least not to this extent. She was more forward, more flirtatious. She was toying with him and teasing him in ways she hadn't before. Alex studied Emily's face. She smiled when his attention shifted to her hair. He noticed something different about it. Before now, she'd always parted it on the side with the rest tucked behind one ear. But as she moved closer to him, he noticed that she had given herself bangs.

Alex brought his fingers up to tuck some of her hair back behind her ear as he had done many times before, but she brushed his hand away.

"What?" Emily asked in a low voice, smiling back at him. "Don't you like it?"

"Yeah, I really do, actually," he said, bringing his hand back up and softly brushing the side of her face. "It's different…sexy."

Emily moved closer still, her nose now practically touching his. She knew that Alex could feel her breath on his face when his pupils dilated, and his breath quickened; she could sense the effect it was having on him. She began gently caressing his lips with her own, teasing him, then pulling back slightly and smiling, her eyes moving from his mouth to his eyes, then back to his mouth. She ran her tongue along his upper lip and watched for his reaction, before softly biting his bottom lip and pulling it gently into her mouth, then letting go.

Running her hand through Alex's hair, she lowered herself onto him, straddling him where he sat on the couch, and pressed her thighs against his. Emily teased him, kissing his neck softly as she pulled his hair, giving her full access to the other side of his neck as she began licking and nibbling his earlobe. She paused to whisper into his ear, describing in surprising detail what she planned to do to him and hoped he would do to her. He slid his hands around her hips and pulled her closer to him.

"Wow! You were never this bold before." Alex exclaimed.

"You're not *upset* with me, are you? If you don't like it, I can stop."

"No," Alex said nervously. "You're good."

"Because… I have a habit of enraging people," Emily whispered in an exaggerated tone. She continued to hold him tightly between her thighs as she lifted her weight off of his lap, placed her hands on the sides of his face and locked eyes with Alex, adding, "but if I ever bore you, it will be with a knife!"

Emily dismounted him as if from a horse and stood in front of him, looking down at his shocked expression, then laughed dismissively as she took another drink of her wine.

"What the fuck, Em!" exclaimed Alex. "What's gotten into you?"

"If I'm being honest, I'm kind of hoping it'll be you," answered

Emily with a smile as she put the glass down and turned toward her bedroom. "Are you coming?" Emily asked as she glanced back at Alex, adding with a wry smile, "Not too soon, I hope." She disappeared into her bedroom.

Alex sat still for a few moments, stunned, then lifted himself off the couch and crept over to the bedroom doorway. As he approached, he could see that Emily was sitting on the side of the bed and that she'd removed most of her clothes. When Alex stopped in the doorway, Emily looked at him with an expression of confusion.

"Why am I in here?" she asked, grabbing at her bedcover and pulling it over her mostly naked body.

Alex moved to the bed and sat beside her, wrapping his arms around her.

"The last thing I remember is moving from the dinner table over to the couch," she said with fear rising in her voice.

"Seriously, Em?" he asked. "You don't have any memory of walking in here?"

Emily shook her head. Alex could feel her tremble. He rubbed her back in an effort to calm her.

"It's okay. Let's just get you into bed," Alex said as Emily slipped under the sheet and cover and laid her head on the pillow.

"Maybe it was too much wine?" suggested Emily, hoping that would be enough of an explanation for what had just happened. "Coming to bed?" Emily asked.

"Yeah," said Alex. "Let me just turn everything off and rinse off the dishes."

Emily nodded, already feeling herself beginning to drift off.

Alex excused himself to go clean up. Emily could hear him take the dishes off the table and the clinking of the wine glasses in the sink.

As the faucet ran in the other room, Emily heard the front doorknob being turned noisily back and forth. Her body tensed, and she lifted her head enough that she could see down the hallway to Alex, who was approaching the front door and peering through the peephole.

As he slowly and quietly backed away from the door, Emily could see that the doorknob was still turning and rattling. Emily knew that Alex was experiencing the same, inexplicable event that she had experienced on several occasions herself. In this moment, however, some kind of heavy force settled over her body, pinning her to the bed, and she found herself unable to move. She tried to call out but no sounds emanated from her mouth despite her frantic efforts. Soon, her head sank back into her pillow for the last time as she plunged into a deep sleep.

* * *

The next morning, Emily awakened feeling strangely more positive. As the sunlight streamed into the apartment from every window, Emily turned her head to see Alex sleeping peacefully next to her. She felt refreshed and wondered if what she had experienced the night before was just some strange dream brought on by Alex's emotional revelations and the wine. As Emily laid in bed staring up at the ceiling, she thought to herself that sunlight truly was the best disinfectant. Still, she was reluctant to delve into whatever may or may not have happened the previous evening, and it was frustrating to her that she could only remember enough about her own behavior that she feared she could expect an embarrassing conversation to follow in the light of a new day. Still, Emily had planned a wonderful day for them to spend together, and she was determined not to let anything spoil that.

* * *

After breakfast, they headed to a local Christmas tree farm, just outside of Rochester, to cut down a tree for Emily's apartment.

As they walked among the trees, they held hands and sipped hot cider, their boots crunching in the snow. Emily was all smiles as she swung Alex's hand back and forth between them.

"Someone is awfully perky this morning," said Alex.

"Of course, I am," said Emily. "It's the holiday season, and we're cutting our first Christmas tree together."

"We've had a tree every Christmas."

"Yeah, I know, but not one we cut down ourselves."

Alex smiled back at Emily. "You're right. I can't argue with stunning logic like that."

Emily let go of Alex's hand and rushed ahead.

"Look at this!" she shouted, running up to a Douglas fir that was taller than she was. "It's perfect."

As she stood next to the tree, she made a sweeping gesture with her arm as if to present the fir to Alex for his consideration.

"Well?" asked Alex.

"What?" responded Emily.

"It's nearly Christmas. You must have some Christmas tree trivia to share."

Emily squealed with delight. "Sure! Let's see…. The Douglas fir has been popular in this country since the 1920s, and it's the perfect Christmas tree because it's got great needle retention."

She paused, thinking.

"Is it all out of your system?"

"For now," she said, smiling.

Alex kneeled at the base of the tree to survey the best angle to cut, then looked back at Emily. "Are you absolutely sure this is the one you want?"

Emily nodded, and Alex put on his gloves, picked up the bow saw he'd borrowed at the entrance to the tree farm, and began sawing down the tree. Once he could feel the tree leaning, he pushed it all the way over, neatened up the cut, grabbed the trunk, and began dragging it through the snow behind him.

"I can take that up to the front for you both," said a farm attendant who had appeared from behind one of the nearby trees.

"That would be great," said Alex pulling off his gloves.

As Emily and Alex walked back up to the entrance to pay for their tree, a vision of the previous night surfaced in Emily's mind.

"Who was at the door last night?" Emily asked.

"The door?"

"Yeah, I thought I saw you looking through the peephole, but then you just backed away, and I must have been dead tired 'cause I don't remember anything after that."

Emily experienced more last night than she was letting on. The cold air seemed to brush the mental cobwebs aside and push last night's weirdness back to the forefront of her memory. She knew she'd need to ease into such a conversation with Alex. She wouldn't normally talk about this, but they had vowed to be more honest and communicative with one another. Plus, she really needed another person's perspective. If this had all really happened last night, and it wasn't just a dream, this would be his first time seeing what she had seen before. If he hadn't seen anything, and this was all truly in her head, she feared that he might make fun of her or think she was crazy, or worse yet, he might realize that he had made a mistake trying to reconcile with her. However, Chloe and Madeleine had seen something. They couldn't all be crazy.

"Oh, that was nothing," said Alex. "I thought I heard someone out in the hallway, but when I looked, there was no one there."

Something *had* happened. Emily wanted to press him further, "You know, there's been a lot of funny stuff happening in that apartment," she said, being careful not to make Alex too uncomfortable to talk about it.

"What do you mean?" he asked.

"Did you sleep as well as I did?" Emily asked, not yet wanting to reveal what had also happened to her.

"Eventually, I guess...yeah," he said kicking an errant twig with his slush covered boot.

"What do you mean, 'I *guess*'?" Emily pressed further.

"Well, how much do you remember from last night? You said some odd things and just were acting a bit more forward than I remember," he shrugged and put his hands in his coat pockets.

"I don't remember taking off most of my clothes if that's what you mean." Emily quipped, as she brushed a few snowflakes off of her scarf.

"Well, you were just a bit flirty, and I probably overreacted, but then you seemed to fall asleep, and it was really peaceful while I cleaned up the kitchen before joining you."

"Okay, but what did you hear in the hallway?"

Taking his hands out of his coat pockets, he stepped closer and put his hands on her shoulders, "I told you. It was nothing.

Now, can we get this tree paid for and back to the apartment? My bits are freezing." Blowing on his hands, he strode off toward the front of the tree farm ahead of her.

Clearly, Emily realized, now was not the time to delve further into the matter. She could tell that Alex was still hesitant to get into what he'd seen, most likely because he didn't want to scare her, but Emily now felt certain that someone, or *something*, had rattled the doorknob in the hallway last night.

The pair made their way to the front of the tree farm, paid for the tree, and watched two of the attendants attempt to lash it to the top of Emily's little car. They rolled down the windows, and looped the rope through, securing the tree as best they could. When the windows were rolled up, the rope was taught. The tree poked out dangerously in front and back of the car. Hopefully, no one would pull them over before they got home.

Soon, they were back in Emily's apartment, enjoying a day filled with Christmas music, hot cider, and laughter together. Emily began hanging ornaments within the branches of her beautiful tree, which was now fully lit up, thanks to Alex, and casting a warming hue within the corner where Emily insisted they place the tree, just next to the front room window.

"Can you hold the other end of this?" Emily asked, holding a snow-white garland in one hand, and extending the other end of it to Alex who was on the other side of the tree. Alex grabbed the end and watched as Emily hung the garland around the tree.

"I kind of liked the *new you*, last night," Alex said, sheepishly.

Emily trained her gaze on the garland, trying not to make eye contact with Alex. "New me? What do you mean?"

She sensed this was the beginning of the embarrassing conversation she'd been dreading. That morning, when Emily had first awakened, she could remember pieces of what had transpired between them, but not enough to fully engage Alex in a conversation about it; not yet at least, and not without worrying him further that there was something really wrong with the apartment – or her.

"I don't know," Alex continued. "You were just really bold, confident, sexy."

'Mortified,' Emily wanted to interject.

"You had me all worked up," Alex continued, "and then you said some really odd stuff. Then you called me into the bedroom; once I moved off the couch to meet you there, you seemed really confused, like you hadn't meant to take off some of your clothes, but I liked the earlier part where you were confident and did what you wanted to me."

She gaped at Alex in stunned confusion, not remembering any of this. Similar gaps in her memory had been happening recently.

"I seem to have these little bits of time that I can't remember. It's been happening more and more frequently. Sometimes, people tell me that my behavior was odd, but I can't remember what they're referring to," she whispered rapidly.

With a sense of concern, Alex suggested, "Look, if you're really worried, maybe you should see a doctor."

Shrugging, Emily said, "I know one thing, I had way too much to drink. I'm sure the doctor would just tell me to drink more responsibly."

She crossed over to the other side of the tree and lightly brushed Alex's arm. He turned to her and bent down to bring himself closer to her, wrapping his arm around her waist.

Emily pressed herself against him and gently kissed his neck, just below his ear, as it was one of the few things she could actually remember doing the previous evening, but then she hesitated and stepped back.

"Let's wait on doing anything further until I can figure this out." Emily suggested, begrudgingly. "Raincheck?" she asked with a smile and raised eyebrows.

Alex let his arms drop. Emily could tell that he was correctly reading her signals. As she looked into Alex's eyes, she could see his disappointment.

"Abso-fucking-lutely," Alex replied with a soft smile.

Emily knew that he could see her disappointment, too. She just needed a little more time.

* * *

Over the rest of that day, the mood of the season helped to cement their bond once again. Alex did eventually open up to Emily about his own inexplicable experience seeing, firsthand, the doorknob on the front door to the apartment turn back and forth – completely on its own – the previous evening. It was the best thing he could have done, for it didn't scare Emily. To the contrary, it was the long-awaited proof from someone other than herself – not just from anyone, but from Alex – that there was in fact something supernatural happening inside her space. The floodgates were finally open, and Emily felt relief that she could tell Alex anything. Moreover, she'd no longer worry that Alex may not believe her. They were talking again and slowly building trust. As Sunday gradually turned into Monday, Alex and Emily woke up refreshed and recharged as they prepared for Alex's morning departure, both feeling certain that the relationship was finally in a good place again.

17

Chloe

"Fuck that guy!" Chloe exclaimed, looking down at her cellphone.

"What now?" asked Emily as she drove them back to the office after lunch.

"Peter just texted *me* an eggplant emoji. Why is he even texting me? I feel like an idiot for letting you pressure me into inviting the little pick to your housewarming party. I only agreed to it because I *thought* he was an *okay guy* and figured he'd be a nice distraction for you to take your mind off…you know, *everything else*."

"Yah, great distraction," Emily said sarcastically, focusing on her driving, "At least it would've been, had I managed to *remember* what we did."

"Well, when I asked him to come over, *because you begged me to*, I hadn't factored in the whole Emily-Pierson-make-out-session that went off in your apartment that night."

"Hey, don't put this back on me," Emily said with a laugh.

"No? Really?" Chloe jibed, "I didn't think, when I asked him to come over, that I was feeding the guy to the lion's den of depravity! He may be an asshole, but after watching you try to perform a tonsillectomy on him with your tongue, I kinda had to feel a little scared for him."

"Shut up!" Emily shouted with exasperation.

"I was afraid for all of us, really. I mean, who were you gonna go after next? Everybody was packed in that tiny apartment of yours like sardines, just watching you two in horror, each of us wondering who was gonna pick the *short straw!*" Chloe continued, further needling Emily.

"Shut. The. Fuck. Up!" Emily shouted back, laughing the whole time.

As they continued to drive back to the office, the mood quieted for a moment; Emily continued to keep her eyes on the road while Chloe stared out her passenger window.

"You know, back when we met in grad school," Chloe said, watching buildings and other sites pass by her field of view as she gazed out the car window, "I had you pegged as the quiet, timid type. A real buzzkill. It took some time for me to warm up to you."

"Yeah, and aren't you glad you did?" Emily said with a smile.

"Absolutely," said Chloe. "Back then, you talked only when you had something you really needed to say. And I just filled up whatever space was left. You gave me plenty of room to stretch out my personality. And you were nice enough to let me boss you around a bit. For your own good, of course."

"Yeah, but you almost killed me that first semester, taking me to every social soiree under the sun."

"Whatever," Chloe dismissed. "At least I tried…."

"And I do appreciate it," Emily said, smiling back at Chloe. "Truly."

Just then, Chloe remembered what brought all of this up in the first place. "Hey," said Chloe, "how come you're not upset by any of this eggplant emoji business with Peter?"

"Peter who?" asked Emily, playfully.

"Um, the guy you – *yuck!* – French kissed the other night," Chloe said. "*That* Peter."

Emily just smiled.

"Wait a minute," Chloe said, exuberantly, as if she'd just solved a riddle. "You and Alex.... Are you back together?"

Emily's smile grew bigger now, and she nodded.

"That is fantastic news, Em! So, when did all this happen? I want every detail!"

Emily paused for a moment. "You don't have to act so surprised...."

"What are you talking about?"

"Alex already told me that you and he were in cahoots."

"Well, I *never!*" Chloe exclaimed, expressing her mock offence with a poor imitation of a southern belle.

They both laughed. It felt great to be the Three Musketeers again.

"Your mom sort of called me," Chloe began, timidly, "after she'd talked to Alex. I reassured her that I'd work on things from my end, so, yah, Alex and I kinda talked a little bit, too."

"Wait a minute," Emily said. "If you were talking to Alex, why'd you even invite Peter to the housewarming? You could have just *not* mentioned anything to him, then told me he had other plans or something"

"Like I said, I wasn't expecting you to throw yourself at the guy in the middle of your party.... I just thought you needed a little fun distraction to boost your confidence until you could pull your head out of your ass and realize you ran off and never let Alex even try to explain what he was up to."

"Not my best moment, I admit."

"Em, Alex worships you. I was ecstatic when he first told me he was interested in you, back in grad school, and I was determined to get you two together. I could see that he was the kind of guy who would understand you."

"Oh, you did, did you?"

"Yeah, I knew he'd be the ideal match for your...*personality*."

"Not another conversation about my personality. Spare me."

"No, not another conversation. It's just...you know, you can be a hard person to get to know. It took the golden child," she said, pointing to herself, "to punch a few holes in that wall of yours. I was so successful that I officially became the third wheel."

"You're no third wheel," Emily insisted. "You're our closest friend."

"I should get the Nobel-fucking-Prize for putting up with you all these years," Chloe laughed.

"Remind me to call Norway when we get back to the office."

"Isn't there a time difference or something? I don't want you to wake those Nobel bastards up in the middle of the night. They're not gonna give me shit if you wake 'em up."

"Come to think about it, I should get some sort of prize myself."

"Why the hell is that?"

"You may not have pursued your dream if it hadn't been for me. I was the one who suggested that you — and whatever that is you call a personality — would be excellent as an on-camera reporter."

"That's true," said Chloe. "And here we are, back together again. Just like old times."

They were silent for a moment.

"We made a great team back then, didn't we?" Chloe asked.

"We did."

"We should work together again," Chloe said, her voice rising. "You know…work up some news packages like we used to in school…. You'll field-produce, and I'll be on-camera."

"To tell you the truth, there are times when I really do miss that," said Emily. "We were really tight together."

"We were…and you didn't even put it down on your resume that you had experience with field producing, Em."

"I know. I should."

As they parked in the station's lot, Chloe took a quick look at her watch.

"Shit!" she said, getting out of the car. "I still have to log bites for the 5 o'clock."

Yet again, Emily thought, watching her friend running ahead into the station building, Chloe would be going down to the wire. Still, despite the numerous occasions when her producer thought she wouldn't have the story ready to air, Chloe consistently proved herself to be one of the best in the business. She was probably faster than anyone at logging the digital material that she and her photographer had captured and then finding the perfect parts of each interview to highlight for the video editors. The editors, in turn, loved working on her stories because she was able to keep everything so well organized in her head. And she could still provide the editors more than their normal due so they could make a quick and easy turn of it and package it for air.

After parking the car and entering the newsroom, Emily saw

Chloe in the edit bay, already deeply engaged in a conversation with one of the editors. A little further down the hall, she could hear someone calling out from the feed room, "Put it up on the bird!" a sort of shorthand for a satellite feed.

The 'feed' room, was where all the satellite links were processed, and various feeds could be plugged in to different rooms in the station or even straight to an individual's office. Emily could usually see several affiliate feeds streaming in the bullpen while she was doing her work, but she seldom paid any attention.

As she passed the feed room, she could see some of her coworkers gathered around one of the monitors. She didn't bother to see what they were watching.

When she reached her desk, she placed her purse into her drawer and returned to the fact-checking assignment she had started before lunch. As she searched through her notes, she could hear the distinctive clip-clopping sound of Chloe's heels entering the bullpen.

"What's going on?" Emily heard Chloe ask one of her coworkers.

The noon-hour floor director, who was standing nearest Chloe, murmured something to her. Emily, trying to focus on her assignment, heard reference to a body being found somewhere. It wasn't unusual for people in the station to gather around the monitors in the bullpen to watch sensational stories like this one. More often than not, they would make inappropriate comments and jokes while they watched. This was a hardened bunch, and several years of working in the industry had left even Emily somewhat hardened, but she chose not to indulge or engage at times like this. However, Emily was unaware, even though the story was being broadcast mere feet from her desk, that another body had been found, this one just twenty minutes from where Emily herself had grown up. As Chloe watched and listened to the coverage, she glanced over at Emily.

Chloe walked towards Emily as the tv blared "Killer in Cherryvale, Kansas."

Emily's head snapped to the television.

18

Sleepover

It had been a challenging day, and Emily, once home, was still reeling from the emotions she felt after hearing the Kansas affiliate news story.

Her mind began to flood with moments from the broadcast:

'...this is what we know at this hour: remains have been exhumed along the edge of a 20-acre parcel near Cedar Springs Lane, just outside of Independence, two hours south-east of Wichita. Authorities have told us that the remains were discovered when the land owner was repairing an irrigation line. We've also confirmed that the remains are that of a child.

'Authorities have continued to try and link several unsolved cases to the Scarecrow Killer for the better part of twenty years. If these remains are determined to be another one of his victims, this would bring the total, so far, to eighteen.'

Emily started to feel uneasy. The news out of Cherryvale reminded her of how she always felt when she began to think of home.

She opened a bottle of her favorite wine and kicked off her shoes. Sitting on her couch, she swirled the glass, sniffed her wine, and took a healthy sip. Something was off. Were there new notes of smoke in her wine? Did she use those glasses for Scotch recently? She checked the label on the bottle. Maybe the year was different from the last bottle she had? Sometimes wine harvested in a fire season has a slightly smokey taste. She swirled and sniffed again. No. The smoke was not coming from the wine. It was in the air. Over the next glass, or two, she kept smelling cigar smoke drifting into her apartment and then dissipating. The building didn't allow smoking, and none of the other tenants smoked at all, let alone cigars. She opened the front window to clear the air and to check if someone was smoking outside the building. She also opened her front door to see if someone was smoking in the hallways. Both proved fruitless. Closing her front door, she was still irritated with the smoke. She started walking around the apartment, sniffing. Maybe something was coming through one of the vents? Turning to the corner of the living room by the window, she saw a faint cloud of smoke. Rushing over to the still open window, she looked out again. Nothing. Looking back, she saw rings of smoke appear a few feet in front of her face as if someone were blowing smoke at her, but there was no one there. The hairs on her neck stood up.

"Hello?" she said. Silence.

She backed away from the corner, waving her hand in front

of her face, watching for it to reappear in the air in front of her. Wide eyed, she felt that creepy feeling of being watched that was starting to become startlingly familiar. She couldn't stay here alone. The medium, Madeleine told her that she shouldn't be afraid, and that was always easier when Chloe was around. She felt ridiculous phoning her closest friend and asking her, once again, to come over and keep her company, but the prospect of spending the night alone in the apartment was much worse. She thought on it and decided that since both Chloe and Alex had promised that they would come over if she needed them, she would make the call.

Emily picked up her phone and scrolled to Chloe's number.

"Chloe, I hate to ask you this, but —"

"Let me guess," Chloe said. "We're doing another sleepover."

"Seriously? You're up for coming over again?"

"To tell you the truth, I was planning to invite myself over there anyway."

"Should I be afraid that you sound so eager to come over all of a sudden?"

"Hmm," said Chloe, pausing to add a little suspense. Then she added with a laugh, "Yeah, probably."

"What do you have up your sleeve?"

"I'm bringing over some technology to record 'irrefutable evidence of the paranormal,' as per the label on the back of the box."

"Are you serious?"

"Oh, I'm serious as a heart attack."

Before Emily could inquire further, Chloe said, "See you in twenty," and quickly hung up.

SLEEPOVER

* * *

In what seemed like no time at all, Emily's phone rang. It was a facetime call from Chloe, so she answered it immediately.

"We're at the car, just outside your building," Chloe said impatiently. Get ready to buzz us in!"

Emily could see that Chloe had some guy she'd never seen before standing next to her, "Who's that with…"

"No time for chit chat, Em," Chloe said, before hanging up on Emily.

Emily ran over to the intercom and pressed it to let Chloe up, and then opened the door slightly so that Chloe could enter on her own. In a few minutes, Chloe pushed past the opened door, carrying an oversized cardboard box stuffed with an assortment of oddly shaped, homemade-looking devices. Following just behind her was the aforementioned stranger who was also carrying an oversized box of even more… 'stuff.' As they each dropped their boxes onto the table, Emily peered into each to see what was inside. Each box appeared to contain various hardware store items, duct-taped together with wires protruding out of them.

"Where did you get all this stuff?" Emily asked, trying to suppress a laugh.

"Kyle, meet Emily," Chloe said, still parting from the load she'd been carrying, "Emily, this is Kyle."

Emily shot Chloe a look that obviously meant to convey that she'd like to speak with her privately.

"Kyle, could you do me a solid and start unpacking some of this stuff for me while I talk to my friend in the other room?" Chloe asked her companion, with a smile and a wink.

Emily grabbed Chloe's hand and pulled her into the bedroom, shut the door, then turned to her friend and began to whisper so as not to have 'Kyle' hear her.

"Who's Kyle?" Emily asked, whispering emphatically.

"He's my brother's roommate," Chloe answered back, sarcastically matching Emily's whispered tone, "and he's got a crush on me." Chloe smiled back at Emily with a shit-eating grin.

"Oh Lord," Emily hissed back, "who doesn't?"

"So anyway… he's really into all this ghost stuff. He's let us borrow some of his equipment to put around your apartment so we can get proof!"

"He's not staying here tonight, is he?"

"No, he's just going to help us set this stuff up."

"Is he going to explain how to use any of this stuff?"

"Yes!" Chloe hissed, "he happens to be a very nice – and extremely smart – guy."

Emily crossed her arms, a little embarrassed that she had questioned such a good deed.

"Well, I must say, it was very sweet of him to drive you over here with all his gear and help us like this," Emily admitted, gingerly, before looking back up at Chloe.

"Oh, and I agreed to take some selfies with him as proof to show his friends that he has some game," Chloe quipped, with a laugh.

"Wow, look at you," Emily replied, "giving a little something to your adoring fans."

"I didn't mind. He's actually kind of cute," Chloe said. "But if you ever tell my brother I said that, I'll kick your ass!"

Chloe opened Emily's bedroom door and motioned her to follow her back out to the main room where Kyle had already begun unboxing his equipment.

"Is everything okay?" asked Kyle.

"We're all good," Chloe answered with a smile, Emily backing her up with a smile of her own.

"So, what does all this do?" asked Emily, eyeing everything that Kyle had laid out on the table to this point.

Kyle reached for one of the devices, "Okay, so this is a REM pod," he began, lifting a small cylinder-shaped object with a retractable antenna extending up from the top that looked as if it had been part of an old RadioShack walkie talkie kit. "I've got two or three of these," Kyle continued.

Chloe noticed that the device had four small glass protuberances extending out from its top.

"What are those," Chloe asked, coquettishly, brushing a finger seductively along one of the bumps.

Emily just watched Chloe and rolled her eyes.

"Those?" Kyle began, "Those are lights. We're going to place these REM pods around the apartment and turn them on. If anyone *or anything* should get close to them, they will light up and beep." Kyle outstretched the antenna on top of the device and switched it on. As he moved his hand within an inch or two of the device, the lights lit up and the device beeped loudly at the three of them.

Emily jumped, slightly, unnerved at the REM pod's unexpected volume.

"Is there anything in that box that doesn't make such a startling noise?" Emily asked with a nervous laugh, before continuing, "can any of this stuff just make evil spirits go away, like those ultrasonic gizmos that repel mice?"

"Afraid not," Kyle answered, "These just collect proof that you're not imagining these things that Chloe says are in your place."

"Can you at least turn the volume down on that thing?"

Chloe suggested, adding "The last thing we're gonna need tonight is to be startled awake by that thing loudly beeping at us."

"No worries," Kyle reassured, gesturing to a small dial affixed to the side, "You can turn them down here."

Chloe then reached into one of the boxes and removed some small devices that looked roughly the size and shape of a deck of playing cards.

"Those are infrared emitters," Kyle began to explain, "They will allow the cameras I brought with me to pick up everything that may be happening throughout your apartment – in complete darkness."

Chloe pulled four tripods from one of the boxes and began to set them up. Kyle followed behind her, placing a small digital camera on each. He then placed two of them in the front room at opposite corners from each other to capture the room from both angles. He placed another to aim down the hall toward the bathroom. Finally, he picked up the last tripod and camera and made his way into Emily's bedroom.

"You and Alex could have some *real* fun with *that* camera set up," Chloe whispered to Emily.

"It's a good thing you're out of earshot of Kyle," Emily hissed, "or I'd have to kill you!"

Emily shot her friend a dirty look, but Chloe didn't seem bothered as she turned back to the table and plucked another item from the box. It looked like something from the hardware store that might test electrical outlets.

"What's that do?" asked Emily, watching Chloe turning it around in her hand."

"It's an EMF meter," answered Kyle, having just made his way back out to the main room, "It detects small changes in electromagnetic energy."

"I have no clue what that means?" said Chloe.

"It will tell you if there's anything in the room with you that you can't see," Kyle began to answer, gingerly attempting to pry the device away from Chloe's ham-fisted grip, "As long as you aren't holding it up to an electrical outlet or anything, you shouldn't expect to pick up any sort of spike in electromagnetic energy."

Kyle outstretched his arm and rotated himself slowly in one spot out in the middle of the room. The meter sat motionless.

"See? Nothing out of the ordinary," Kyle explained in a reassuring tone, "If, however, you *do* get a spike, it may indicate that something is here with you."

"Wonderful" Emily sighed, taking the device from Kyle and placing it back on the table, as one might take a toy from a child to get them to stop playing with it.

"Okay, well, I guess that's everything," Kyle said, scanning the living room, "I've also placed digital audio recorders in each room. If there's anything paranormal in here, we should capture evidence of it."

Chloe took him by the elbow and led him to the front door.

"Thank you for your help, Kyle. We really appreciate it."

"Yes, thank you, Kyle!" Emily called from across the room.

"My pleasure," he said uncertainly as Chloe gave him a gentle push into the hallway. "Please don't break any of my equip—" The word was clipped by the sound of the closing door.

Chloe locked the door, turned, and leaned up against it, looking back at Emily.

"I'll tell you one thing," Chloe whispered with a grin, "I'm not about to remove a stitch of my clothing tonight with these frickin' night-vision cameras all over the place. The last thing

I need is for Kyle to see me naked on his ghost equipment – or worse, my brother!"

* * *

At 3:33 a.m., Emily was jolted awake from another nightmare.

In the dream, she was a little girl, of middle school age. She was in a basement with a childhood friend, and they were looking for something, but she couldn't remember what. When she turned to say something to her friend, her friend's eyes appeared grey, as if she had been dead for some time. The friend just stood there, lifeless, gazing past her with those blank, soulless eyes. Emily started to run upstairs, but she could feel that something had grabbed her and started to pull her back. She glanced back to see that it was her friend pulling her back down the stairs. As she struggled to get away, the girl, who still had a grip on her, started to scream. As she did so, her mouth gaped open in an inhuman way, like her jaw had detached from the rest of her skull, and Emily felt powerless to do anything else but scream hysterically.

Now fully awake, her heart pounding, she turned to see if her movement had awakened Chloe. It hadn't. Emily lay in bed, looking up at the ceiling and breathing slowly and deeply to regain her sense of calm. Emily felt herself drifting back to sleep, but she also felt the need to pee, so she slid herself from the bed and shuffled into the bathroom.

As she sat, on the verge of drifting off to sleep again, she heard a buzzing noise from the main room. It was one of the REM pods. SHIT! Her first thought was that Kyle clearly neglected to turn the dam buzzers down – or off, as she had asked him to do; then she was overcome with the fear that such a loud noise would annoy her neighbors. Her walls seemed to be paper-thin at the most inconvenient times. Any feelings of drowsiness were gone in an instant. She quickly finished up in the bathroom then made her way down the hall to the main room so that she could turn off the sound before her neighbors would complain. In that moment, with her rushing to turn off the noise, it hadn't even occurred to her that the device might have gone off for the intended reason it was set out there in the first place. The room was dimly lit by the streetlights in front of the apartment building. The soft glow of the lamps shone through the room's uncovered windows.

Emily saw Chloe's silhouette gazing out one of the windows. She must have awakened her when she got out of bed, but before she could apologize, she realized that it wasn't Chloe. In the soft, low light, she recognized the woman with the unmistakable blunt bob. Emily was fascinated as she watched Louise stand there, her arms crossed in front of her as she gazed pensively into the night. A light snow was falling, and the flakes were catching the light from the streetlights; Emily could see them through the window, too. This was not the young girl who had previously visited her. This was Louise in her heyday, when she was eighteen or nineteen years old. Emily knew Louise was just a little over five feet tall, but she felt her presence fill the room. Emily could now see that she wore a lovely silk kimono robe, and beneath that, her pajama bottoms were long enough to completely cover her feet. They, too, were a shimmering silk.

Emily saw Louise's hair catching the light from the streetlights outside. It couldn't be Louise Brooks standing at her window, she thought, because it just couldn't be. Yet it was her, fully solid, exactly as she had seen the child at her door. As the young woman pressed her face against the window, her breath began to fog the glass. Seeing her this way, so real, Emily could understand why she had captivated so many.

The apparition turned her gaze to Emily. Even in the low light, Emily could see that none of the photographs she had seen of Louise had fully captured her striking beauty.

Louise acknowledged Emily, smiled at her and winked. Emily stood still, watching her slowly vanish. The room seemed darker after she was gone. Emily kept looking where Louise had stood, wiping tears from her eyes. She took a deep breath, realizing in that moment, that she hadn't even noticed that the REM pod had stopped buzzing at almost the instant she saw the apparition. She moved across the room, quietly, then knelt down to pick up the REM pod so she could turn it off. Bringing it up closer so she could see it more clearly in the light of the window, she could see that it was turned off already. Emily wondered, had Kyle failed to turn it on? He'd absolutely done so, Emily remembered; he showed them both how it reacted when he moved his hand near it. Who or what turned it off, she wondered. She gained her composure as best she could, then she returned to her room and crawled back under the covers. Louise was all she could think about now.

Emily looked over at Chloe, who was still asleep. She nudged her friend.

"Are you awake?" Emily whispered. There was no response. Emily nudged Chloe harder and whispered again, "Are you awake?"

"I am now," Chloe said, annoyed. "What the hell."

"I just saw Louise again," Emily whispered.

"Where? At the front door again? What woke you up?"

"I heard the REM buzzer when I was in the bathroom and

went out to shut it off. And then, I saw her out in the front room," Emily explained. "She was just standing there, looking out the window. And she wasn't a child this time. This was the Louise we know from the movies."

"You gotta be shittin' me! Wait, but I would have heard the buzzer, too. Why didn't I wake up?"

Emily shrugged.

Chloe flung the covers off herself and hopped over Emily onto the floor, running out to the front room.

Emily listened to Chloe from the bedroom.

"I don't see anything out here now. The REM buzzer thing is turned off. Are you sure you didn't turn it off when you were out here?" Chloe said.

Then Emily could hear Chloe open the refrigerator door.

"I'm gonna make a mess of this pie," Chloe said. "You want anything?"

"No, thanks."

As the refrigerator door closed, Emily heard Chloe scream.

Emily jumped from the bed, ran to the front room, and flipped on the light. Chloe was standing with her back against the kitchen counter, her eyes wide. The remains of the pie lay upside down on the floor. Emily ran over to Chloe and grabbed hold of her.

"What happened?" Emily asked.

Chloe couldn't speak. Her heart was racing, and Emily could feel her shaking.

"It's okay now," said Emily, holding Chloe's face in her hands and looking straight into her frightened eyes.

"I opened the fridge to get out the pie, and when I closed it, there was a giant, black figure standing behind the fridge door!" Chloe whisper-yelled with tears in her eyes.

Just then, a noise emanated from the bedroom.

Emily dashed inside her room and switched on the light. She watched as the closet doorknob slowly turned back and forth. Her eyes widened, and she rushed back into the main room, where Chloe stood, terrified and gazing at the front door.

That door, too, was rattling, and there was the sound of something on the other side of it, pounding to try to get in. They could both see the front doorknob begin to twist, as if someone on the other side were testing to see whether the door was locked.

Emily approached the door with caution and peered through the peephole. Despite the door still shaking, Emily could see that there was no one in the hall.

"Come on, Chloe. Let's go!" Emily yelled, quickly unlocking the dead bolt and throwing open the front door as she leaped out of the apartment into the corridor, Chloe close behind her.

They rushed to Hazel's apartment and pounded on the door. "Hazel, it's Emily, could you please just let us in. Hurry!"

From the other side, they could hear Hazel calling out, "I'm coming, I'm coming."

Hazel opened the door and was almost knocked down as Emily and Chloe raced past her into the apartment.

"Oh, my," Hazel said, closing and locking the door. "What on earth is the matter, dears?"

Before either of them could say anything, Hazel's front door began shaking violently.

19

Pandora's Box

Hazel stepped back from the door. "My word!" she said, raising her voice over the noise. "Whoever you are," she said, facing the door, "you'd better move along, or I'll call the police."

Suddenly, the noise at the front door stopped.

"Whoever they were, they seem to have gone now," said Hazel.

She turned to Emily and Chloe. "Who is following you at this hour of the morning?" Hazel asked. "Are you all right? Are either of you hurt?"

"No, I think we're both okay, Hazel," Emily said. "Just give us a moment to catch our breath."

Hazel tightened her robe and went over to her favorite chair to sit.

"It's okay, dear," Hazel replied gently. "You can tell me if it was a terrible drug deal gone bad or something. You know, the guy in 302 is putting something up his nose, I'm just sure of it."

Chloe, although still terrified, couldn't help but giggle. Hazel glanced across at Chloe, as if Chloe had just confirmed her suspicions.

"We had another really bad scare at my apartment," Emily explained. "Thanks for letting us in."

"It's no trouble at all, child," Hazel responded, a small laugh in her voice. "I was up anyway. You know us old people; we eat dinner at three in the afternoon, go to bed by eight-thirty, and then we're up at four in the morning."

Chloe and Emily exchanged a glance, smiling slightly.

"Besides, when you're as old as I am, you've pretty much seen it all," Hazel said. She paused for a moment to gather her thoughts before continuing. "I don't recall anybody else having this kind of issue inside your apartment."

"So, this whole door thing is new to you, too?" asked Emily.

"Yes," Hazel replied. "I think it's the first time for any of us in this building. I've known all the other tenants who lived in your apartment…. If there was anything that terrible going on in there, I'm sure I would have heard about it."

"I'm not lying about any of it," Emily said.

"Oh, no, dear. I'm not suggesting anything of the kind. All I'm saying is that apart from me, no one else other than you had seen anything unusual in the building, and no one has ever said anything about threatening supernatural occurrences in your apartment."

"Seriously?" Chloe asked.

"When she showed me the locket and told me about the young girl who came to see her," Hazel said, addressing Chloe now, "I knew right then and there that our Emily was special. In thirty-plus years, not a soul ever said anything — to me or anyone else in this building — about seeing a little girl with bobbed hair."

"She visited me tonight. I saw her in my front room, and then all hell broke loose. What does she want from me?" Emily wondered.

"She must see something in you, I suppose," Hazel said. "Perhaps it's something profoundly intimate you both share."

Hazel rose from her chair. "Can I get you two some coffee?" Hazel asked. "It's freshly made."

The pair nodded, and Hazel went to the kitchen to get a few cups from the cabinet.

"I was going to come over and visit you today," Hazel said as she poured coffee into one of the cups. "I found something I thought you would appreciate."

Hazel finished up in the kitchen and took the two cups into the main room, placing them on the coffee table in front of Emily and Chloe, next to her own cup.

"Chloe, dear?" Hazel began, a little winded, "Would you be a dear and bring that box over here that I placed on the side table next to the front door?"

Chloe rose from the couch and made her way over to the table where Hazel had placed an old-looking wooden box.

"I was looking through my things and discovered something that belonged to Louise," Hazel said, smiling at Emily with anticipation.

Hazel reached out to Chloe and retrieved the box, carefully putting it in front of Emily, allowing her to view the torn label that covered much of the exterior. It looked to be very old and worn. As Emily moved forward to get a better look at Hazel's curiosity, she could see what appeared to be a vintage wooden cigar box, roughly ten inches by twelve inches and perhaps five or six inches tall. Emily could see that the top lid had a latch on the front in order to keep it from opening. The lid was inscribed with the words "RANNEY ALTON MERCANTILE — HIGH FIVE," and it depicted five bowler-hatted gentlemen, each in his own ornately flourished oval frame.

"May I have a look?" Emily asked.

"Of course, darling."

Emily gently picked up the box, noticing the year 1913 etched on one of the inner edges. She rotated the box in her hands to see the antique artwork on the box's sides. She placed the box on her lap and gingerly opened the top, her eyes widening as she examined the photos and trinkets within.

"That box belonged to Louise," Hazel said.

"Oh...," Emily said, feeling a rush of emotion.

"Of course, it was her father's first. Louise said he enjoyed a cigar on special occasions, and he always had them on hand to offer to his clients."

Emily noted the faint odor of tobacco rising from the open box. She flashed to earlier that night when her apartment was filled with a similar aroma.

"When she was a young girl," Hazel said, "she'd put her most prized things in there. Then she'd hide it under her bed so her brothers or younger sister wouldn't find it. Later, I suppose it became a place for her to bury her Kansas baggage."

"'Kansas baggage'?" Chloe asked.

"That was her term for it," Hazel said. "She was embarrassed that she grew up in Kansas. As much as she probably would have liked to, she couldn't escape who she was. That box became a special home for items she either loved or couldn't bear the thought of throwing away. She tended to punish herself, so she also saved things that reminded her of her failures and regrets. You'll see there's more in there than just items from her childhood in Kansas."

"I can relate," Emily replied.

Hazel just sat silently and smiled.

"That locket of yours was in that box until quite recently. I'm not sure how she did it, but she found a way to connect with you come hell or high water," Hazel said. "I believe she treasured that locket, but I think it represented her painful relationship with her parents. She loved them, I know, but I don't think they had time for her, and when she needed them most, they didn't protect her."

Emily saw a printed pamphlet in the box and took it out to study it more carefully. In the photograph on the cover, Louise appeared to be in her thirties. Although she still wore bangs, her hair was shoulder length in the photo, and her style of clothing, a white shortened topcoat and long black pants, appeared closer to that of the late 1930s or early 40s. The photo captured Louise in a ballet pose. The title of the pamphlet was *The Fundamentals of Good Ballroom Dancing*.

"Interesting," Emily said, flipping through the pamphlet.

"Yes, but I think, for Louise, it represented another failure," Hazel said.

"Failure? Why?"

"After leaving Hollywood for the final time," Hazel said, "she returned to Wichita and tried her hand at operating a dance studio. She had to close within two years. She wrote that guide while her studio was still in operation. After it failed, she left Kansas for good, and I don't believe she ever wanted to look back."

Emily pulled one of the pictures from the pile and examined it carefully. It was a photograph of a young Louise standing with a few adults in front of a lovely Victorian home. A dull ache began to grow at her temple.

"She was one of the Brooks' Cherryvale neighbors," Hazel said, pointing to the lady standing closest to Louise. "That's Mrs. Strickler, Louise's other mother, the one we spoke about."

Emily's gaze was drawn to one of the other adults in the picture, a man dressed in overalls who seemed out of place in the image. He was standing off to the side and behind the others, like an afterthought.

Emily's head was flooded with images. She knew him, but how? She could hear his voice digging into her skull.

Chloe could see that something was wrong.

"What's the matter?" Chloe asked.

"I'm not sure," Emily replied, her palm firmly on her forehead.

"That," Hazel said, pointing at the man in the photo. "That's Mr. Flowers."

Emily let go of the photo as if she'd discovered it was on fire. She quickly closed the box and pushed it off her lap and back onto the table in front of her.

"Let me get you something cool to drink, dear," Hazel said, rising from her chair.

Chloe picked up the photo and looked at the man in the background. "What's the deal with this Mr. Flowers?"

"That's the man who molested Louise," Hazel said, setting a glass of water beside Emily.

"Wait a minute," Chloe replied, returning her attention to Emily. "Did you know about this guy?"

"Hazel told me about him before, but I didn't know there was a picture of him."

"But you felt something as soon as you held up the photo,"

Chloe said. "It was almost as if you were responding to it before Hazel had a chance to tell you who was in the picture."

Hazel shifted her gaze to Chloe. Her expression indicated that she suspected more, but that she felt it was not her place to speak for Emily.

"What am I missing here?" Chloe asked.

Emily buried her face in her hands. She'd never admitted this to anyone else before, and she found it difficult to say out loud.

"Something happened to me, too…when I wasn't much older than Louise," Emily said.

A look of shock and helplessness began to wash over Chloe's face.

"Oh, my God, I'm so sorry, Em" Chloe said softly as she moved closer to console her friend. "You were…?"

"I'm not sure…. I mean, I can't remember," Emily said, groaning in frustration. "There's only fragments, bits and pieces…. I think I mainly shut everything out, but every now and again something will just bring it up again."

"Did you tell anyone?" Chloe asked cautiously. "You know, when it happened?"

"No, I've never told anybody…. Not even my parents. What would I have told them? I'm not even sure of the details. Yet certain things will set it off. Those things Louise told me at my door on Halloween. These disturbing dreams I've been having. The photo in that box. It's all coming together. And it's overwhelming."

Hazel looked on with empathy, a sense of confirmation in her eyes.

"Emily, you need to talk to someone about this," Chloe said gently. "You can't bottle this up. You need some help."

"The night that Madeleine Bloom came over.... I didn't say anything, but she brought something up."

"What did she say?" Chloe asked.

"Do you remember when she mentioned the crawl space?"

"Yeah."

"I don't think that had anything to do with Louise," Emily said, taking a deep breath. "I think it had to do with me."

20

Digging a Hole

He'd been shoveling for what felt like an hour when he decided to take another break. He was far enough away from town to be certain that no one would notice what he was doing out here. He leaned on the shovel and peered down at the hole, unsure if it was deep enough. A dog began to bark in the distance; he looked up to see if anybody was around. The barking ceased, and only the repetitive chirping of crickets could be heard.

He decided he wanted the hole to be a little deeper, so he raised the shovel up, slamming it back into the ground with enough power to drive it into the soil a few more inches. He despised this part of the process. It was exhausting work, and he'd grown tired of having to do things this way. It was a terrific motivation for him to do better the next time, he thought. It all started to feel like a ludicrous waste of time and effort, especially given the minimal satisfaction achieved. Everything happened too quickly.

He'd spend weeks selecting his target. And to do so without raising suspicion had almost become an art form unto itself. At the very least, that aspect was becoming easier, and if he was being completely honest, it had developed into one of his favorite parts. It gave him a feeling of power when he would outwit his victims. However, the end still came too soon.

He paused from his digging once again to recover his breath and wipe the sweat from his brow. Fuck this, he decided. I can restrain them in the basement and enjoy them for a much longer period of time. He could add some further soundproofing to ensure he wasn't heard. And there was rope and wire and such to keep them still.

He examined the hole once more and determined that it was sufficiently deep. He set his shovel beside the pit and strolled back to the car, where he unlocked the trunk. He studied the small, lifeless body he'd wrapped in a painter's tarp. He was amazed at how much more adept he had become at duct taping the entire mass into the shape of a cocoon. He'd found that the trick was to put out the tarp first and then have his fun. It was far simpler than laying everything out afterward and then attempting to pull the corpse onto it. This way, he could roll it up like a sleeping bag, sling it over his shoulder, and quickly load it into the trunk of the car.

He picked up his bundle and walked up to the hole, dumping it in with a thump. He was right to dig a bit deeper. It was an ideal fit. He took the shovel and began filling the hole. Within a few minutes, he lost sight of anything beneath the earth, and the hole had almost vanished. The final task was to kick some of the surrounding leaves over the top with his boot.

He was finished.

He glanced at his watch, pleased that he had completed this chore in the shortest time yet. It was time to return to town...and home.

21

Despair

The next morning, Emily felt the warmth of the early morning sunshine on her face as it shone through Hazel's front window. She opened her eyes with a squint and picked up her cell phone to see the time. It was 8:15 a.m.

For a moment, Emily thought she was scheduled for work, but then she remembered it was her day off. It was Friday, and Alex would be arriving later that afternoon to stay the weekend.

She glanced over at Chloe, who was still slumped over on her side of the couch, asleep, then turned her attention to Hazel, who was silently reading in her favorite armchair.

Emily nudged Chloe awake. Chloe rubbed the sleep from her eyes and propped herself upright on the couch.

"Who wants to go out to breakfast?" Emily asked. "My treat!"

Emily felt terrible for barging into Hazel's apartment hours earlier, and although she was relieved that Chloe could now corroborate her reports of paranormal activity, Emily also felt awful for dragging her friend into *her* problem. Worse, she felt no closer to fixing the situation. This meant that she would have to continue relying on people around her, which made her feel weak and dependent.

They went downtown for breakfast. The trip provided not only the ideal excuse to stay away from the apartment for a little while longer but also a delicious meal and comfortable conversation. Emily felt lighter, as though the bright morning swept the darkest thoughts from her mind. Kyle had said that he'd review the digital footage and let them know if it had picked up anything, so Emily and Chloe agreed to return to Emily's apartment later that morning to collect the equipment they'd set up the night before and return it to him. First, though, they would enjoy their meal together.

* * *

They arrived back at Emily's apartment building, ready to begin the task of breaking down the tripods and other paranormal equipment and packing everything back into the boxes Kyle had left behind. After Emily parked the car in the garage and turned the engine off, the three of them sat for a moment; Emily and Chloe were trepidatious about having to go back into that apartment.

"Should we all go up there together?" asked Chloe. "Strength in numbers, you know."

"If you don't mind, dears," Hazel interjected, "I think I'll sit the rest of this little adventure out, but if you need me, I'm always just down the hall."

The pair thanked Hazel again for letting them crash at her place as they all got out of the car. From the garage, they made their way through the laundry area to the lobby. As she pulled out her keys, peering into the lobby, Emily recalled the feelings she'd had months earlier when she first visited the building. She remembered her eagerness to see the apartment in person after spending so much time reviewing pictures of it online. As she and her companions made their way to the elevator, she began to think about the figure she thought she'd seen in the bedroom window, from outside the apartment, during that first visit. She had reasoned to herself, then, that what she'd seen must have been a trick of the light and the reflections on the window outside. Now, however, she knew that what she'd seen up in that bedroom window *was* indeed a figure. Moreover, she'd been cohabitating with whatever that thing was – this entire time – and she felt her dread crystalize into a gnawing pit, threatening to overwhelm her.

They rode the elevator to the third floor and stepped out into the hall. After pausing for a moment, they walked down the hallway to Hazel's apartment and made sure she got in safely, then walked back over to apartment 307. Before inserting her key, Emily leaned close to the door, listening. Hearing nothing, she unlocked the door and pushed on it, letting it swing open as they remained in the hall. The apartment was in shambles. Emily's Christmas tree was lying on its side in the middle of the floor. The couch was upended and leaning against one of the corners. All the kitchen drawers were open, and silverware was spread all over the floor.

"Holy shit!" Chloe exclaimed.

Emily took a first step into her apartment, cautiously walked to her bedroom doorway, and peeked into the room. It, too, looked as though it had been ransacked. The closet door was wide open, and clothing had been thrown onto the floor. Emily's bed covers were completely stripped and were lying in a bundle in front of the bed.

"I'm just going to get all this stuff back into the boxes so we can get out of here," Chloe said, moving to one corner of the room to collect and collapse one of the tripods.

Emily felt violated as she looked around her apartment. As she examined the rooms, she was struck by how much of it seemed to have been done in a fit of anger. The scale of the violence sent a familiar chill down her spine.

"All of this happened after we went to Hazel's apartment" Emily acknowledged, glancing back at Chloe, "I'm curious whether those cameras captured any of it."

Chloe nodded her head in agreement; she was uncharacteristically quiet, looking around, and behind herself, as if to make sure nothing would advance on her from behind. As Emily carefully climbed over a pile of debris to get into her bedroom, Chloe continued disassembling the tripods and rounding up other items she and Kyle had set up in the room.

Emily continued to survey the damage. She wondered if there was any rhyme or reason to the items that got tossed around or destroyed, but she couldn't find any evidence of an attempt to communicate anything other than to throw a tantrum – or simply to scare her. Then something came to mind; the entire apartment looked as if a twister had gone through it. Being a Kansas native, Emily knew all too well what the aftermath of a tornado looked like, and she began to wonder if *that itself* was the message. Was all of this a massive show of strength to acknowledge her Cherryvale connection? Was this display intended for Louise, too? In her visitation last night, she had attempted to present herself in a completely non-threatening manner. Her visitation expressed warmth and calm. That, too, may have pissed this thing off. Yes, Emily decided, this was a message. This thing was threatened that she and Louise had made a connection.

After Chloe placed all the equipment together, Emily helped her stuff the equipment back into the boxes she and Kyle had brought. Each of them took a box and slowly, carefully, backed their way out of the apartment. On their way out, Emily made sure to lock the door behind her.

As they were loading the box into the trunk, Emily asked, "Do you think Alex and I could come stay with you tonight, Chloe?"

"Are you kidding me? Of course," said Chloe. "You're not going back in there until we get some answers...and reinforcements!"

* * *

They arrived at Chloe's brother's apartment, and Chloe let them in with the unauthorized copy she'd made of her brother's key.

"Wyatt!" Chloe shouted, as she peeked into her brother's apartment, hoping to rouse him from his bedroom. "I hope you're wearing pants!"

Wyatt leaned out from his bedroom. "So did you catch anything with that stuff, or did it all end up being a big dud?"

Chloe spoke before Emily could respond.

"Just come out here, already," said Chloe. "Where's Kyle?

Chloe's brother backed into his room, and they could hear him stumbling about, presumably to make himself more presentable.

"Kyle!" Wyatt bellowed from his own bedroom, "Your girlfriend's here."

Kyle peeked out from his room, then both he and Chloe shouted back at her brother in tandem, "Shut up, Wyatt!"

Chloe turned her gaze back at Kyle, giving him a subtle nod and a wink, "What's up, Kyle."

Emily rolled her eyes.

"Does that actually work on guys?" Emily whispered to Chloe, giggling.

"Look at me. What do *you* think?" snapped Chloe in a whisper, then smiling back at Emily, "He's cute, right?"

Emily smiled and shook her head. At the very least, Chloe's absurd flirting with her younger brother's roommate provided a welcome diversion.

It didn't take long for Kyle to make himself presentable in order to make his suave entrance for Chloe's benefit. By contrast, Wyatt took a little longer to make his way out of his room; Emily figured Wyatt wasn't in any hurry to impress this particular friend of his older sister, especially since she was more like an older sister to Wyatt. Emily had known him since he was just a kid.

As Kyle began pulling the small cameras from the boxes and removing the SD card from each, being careful to note which card came from which camera, Chloe and Emily watched him intently. It was almost mesmerizing to watch the skill with which he seemed to hold command over his workspace. Wyatt placed the first SD card into the slot on his computer, brought up the video, and began to scan it for anything.

"This footage is from one of the two cameras that were placed to capture the main room," Kyle announced as he fast-forwarded through the footage, looking for anything anomalous.

"Want something to eat, Em," Chloe said with a nudge before making her way to the kitchen.

"You're hungry again?" asked Emily with disbelief, "We just had breakfast not an hour ago."

"I know, the stress is making me hungry. Wyatt!" Chloe shouted at her brother who still hadn't come out of his room yet, "What do you got to eat around here?"

Wyatt's voice yelled back at his sister from the other room, "There's sesame chicken from the restaurant. It's in the fridge"

Chloe opened the fridge and looked inside, "How old is it?"

"It's from last night," Wyatt yelled back at her, "Just eat it, fool!"

Chloe looked at Emily, "I don't trust him, but I don't care anymore. I'm going for it."

She removed the glass dish from the refrigerator and placed it on the counter in front of her.

"You want any of this?" Chloe asked Emily.

"Thanks. I'm good," Emily smiled back as she watched Chloe place the chicken into the microwave.

"Wait, what?" Kyle said, not taking his eyes off the screen. "Duuuuude, are you shittin' me right now? Is this for real?"

Emily glanced back at computer monitor as Chloe ran from the kitchen over to the table to see what Kyle was looking at. Even Wyatt had come out of his room to see what was going on. Kyle paused the video and wiped it backward for a few seconds before pressing the play button again. They all watched the footage they'd recorded, which seemed to show Emily's dining table sliding across the floor *on its own*. They all gasped when an eight-foot-tall black mass suddenly appeared onscreen as a shadow, crossing the room and then leaving the frame. In that instant, one of the kitchen drawers slid open, and the silverware shot out, scattering cutlery across the room.

"Whoa!" Kyle said. "Were you sleeping when all this was going on?"

"No," said Chloe, "This all happened after we left her apartment. We'd had our fill of that place, long before this stuff happened"

For the next thirty minutes, the group remained glued to Wyatt's display. With a few exceptions, there was practically nonstop activity inside Emily's apartment.

"Have you tried listening to any of the recorders yet?" Kyle asked.

Chloe and Emily shook their heads. Kyle grabbed the recorder that had been placed in Emily's bedroom, plugged his headset into it, and began to listen intently.

Chloe and Emily moved back over to the Kitchen where Chloe pulled the sesame chicken form the microwave and opened the lid to check on it. Emily kept her eye on Kyle, half hoping he wouldn't hear anything from the digital audio recordings.

"You sure you don't want any of this?" Chloe asked Emily once more.

"Thanks, but no. I'm good," Emily responded, still watching Kyle intently.

Chloe grabbed some chopsticks from one of the kitchen drawers and began to tweeze a morsel from the glass bowel into her mouth.

"The way you're staring at him," Chloe whispered, sarcastically, "I'd think you were into him."

"Shhhh! I'm trying to hear what's going on."

"How can you hear anything, Em? He's got his headphones on."

"Would you just shut up?" Emily hissed back.

"Guys, you should hear this," Kyle shouted. He removed the headphones from his ears and routed the sound from the digital recorder to his computer to take advantage of the larger speaker. After a few seconds of quiet, the group heard words they couldn't quite make out being uttered in a harsh whisper.

Emily shuddered. "It sounds so evil."

"What did that just say?" Chloe asked sharply. "Can you play it back?"

Kyle rewound the recording a few seconds and then pressed play again.

They all huddled around to listen carefully. This time, there was no mistaking the words:

"You'll end up like the rest of them...dead in the basement."

Emily froze with fear. She'd heard this threat before, not just at Halloween but long before, from a man she thought she knew and trusted.

Suddenly, Emily felt the blood drain from her face, and she grew dizzy. The light on the table next to Wyatt seemed to swing like the light on the cord had swung in that damp, musty room. She fell into darkness.

22

Nightmares

Emily awoke in Chloe's bed. She didn't remember being taken back to Chloe's apartment. She wondered how long she'd been out; it must have been hours, she realized, because she could hear Alex and Chloe in the other room, and she knew the drive from Chelsea was nearly five hours. She wanted to tell Alex what had happened and show him some of the footage they'd captured with Kyle's equipment. She wanted to…, but she was still too drowsy to put words together in any intelligible way. Emily, terrified, was left to wonder how she could ever go back to that apartment after receiving so much concrete proof that it was haunted. And the disturbances had clearly escalated. Still groggy, Emily slipped back out of consciousness, but her sleep was quickly replaced by vivid nightmares.

* * *

Mary rushed down the stairs and swung herself around the banister, almost colliding into Mrs. Strickler, who'd been calling for her to taste some fudge she'd been cooling on the counter.

"Mary Louise Brooks!" Mrs. Strickler said, startled by the little one who had practically fallen into her and taking hold of the girl's shoulder to prevent her from running by. "You're liable to slip and fall if you're not more careful."

"Yes, Aunt Tot," said Mary, respectfully.

"The fudge is on the countertop, sweetheart," said Mrs. Strickler. "If you like that batch, I'll teach you how to make some of your very own."

As she dashed into the kitchen, she caught sight of herself in one of the glass-front cabinet doors. She snatched a piece of fudge from the platter and stared at her reflection as she savored each mouthful of the moist, chewy sweet.

As the scene flashed into Emily's consciousness, she could see herself running across the hardwood flooring of a beautiful Victorian home. She understood that this was not Louise's home, but the home of the Stricklers. She glanced up to see Mr. Flowers standing two or three rungs up on a wooden ladder, wiping away some excess paint from one of the door trims. He looked directly at Louise, and in so doing, he stared directly into Emily's eyes.

A bright light flashed, and Emily looked up to see that she was now in a dimly lit room. She glanced down and noticed her shoes — the patent leather shoes that Mary had worn. She felt pressure and looked at her sides. She saw enormous hands that held her tightly in place. When she heard his voice and looked up, she was staring into the eyes of Mr. Flowers. He pulled her closer to him, and she could smell the tobacco on his breath.

> *"You're quite pretty,"* Mr. Flowers said, his grip on her arms enough to leave bruising. *"But you'd better keep those pouty little lips shut, or you're gonna end up dead in the basement."*

Emily awoke with a start. Her head pounding, she was trembling, and she was frustrated that these dreams had been coming to her so much more frequently recently. She called out to Chloe who was in the other room.

"Do you have anything to calm my nerves?"

"Sure, Em," Chloe replied, poking her head into the darkened bedroom, "I've got some strong cold medicine that should work, especially if you chase it with some whiskey."

Chloe was gone only a few seconds and then returned, medicine in hand. She handed it over to Emily and said, "Go on back to sleep; we're fine out here. I've been showing Alex some of the footage that I recorded from Kyle's computer onto my phone."

Chloe's voice drifted in and out of Emily's consciousness. Unable to respond, Emily's eyes closed, and her head hit the pillow.

* * *

Emily's visions flashed again. She could see herself now, not Louise anymore.

> *She was in a dark basement, and she'd been thrown to the floor with great force. She could hear heavy boots on wood, and she glanced up to see a man bounding back up the stairs. He slammed the door behind him, and she could hear the door being locked from the other side. As her eyes began to adjust, she could see that she was within a damp, musty room, its walls made of cinder blocks. The room was illuminated by only a low-wattage bulb hanging from a single cord that was nailed up to one of the joists. Out of the corner of her eye, she glimpsed something wrapped in plastic in the corner. As she got nearer, she could see a little girl, wrapped completely in plastic, immobile, with her wrists bound, and her eyes fixed in a blank stare. In that moment, although she was just 12 years old herself, she knew that what she was looking at was the gruesome remains of a little girl's body.*

Although too young to completely comprehend what had happened to this girl at the time, Emily's adult self understood exactly what had happened to this girl; blood was splattered throughout the plastic she'd been rolled into. This man had locked her in this basement, probably raped her, and then killed her. Moreover, Emily knew that he'd be coming back down those stairs again soon — for her.

> *She gained her composure enough to pull herself along the wooden railing and slowly climb the stairs. She was*

in a lot of pain and winced with each step. She paused several times to wipe the tears from her face and take slow, deep breaths.

"You're just another silly bitch like the other ones!" said the gruff voice on the other side of the door. "Don't try anything stupid, little piggy piggy, or you'll end up like the rest of them!"

Emily froze and waited until she heard his boots fade away. She waited a few minutes more to be sure he had left, and then she grabbed the doorknob and tried to turn it back and forth, panicking. It was locked. She slammed herself against the door with all her might, but the door didn't budge. She pushed at it over and over.

She heard the heavy tread of boots rushing back towards her. The man on the other side of the door spoke again, "Those people on the news, they don't know what they're talking about," he said. "Scarecrow didn't need a brain. Dumb bitches. I'll find an extra-special place to bury you, piggy, but I'll make sure you're still alive when I do it!"

Emily made her way back down the old wooden stairs and scanned her surroundings for a way out.

Emily's mind flashed again. This time, she was on the floor of the basement, and the man was on top of her.

She couldn't bear to look directly at him, so she stared into the darkness of the top edges of the cinder block walls; she started counting blocks to try to distract herself. While counting, her eyes traced down the wall until she caught another glimpse of the little girl's body as it lay in a darkened corner of the basement. She looked into the girl's dead, lifeless eyes and tried, again, to mentally remove herself from this horrible event. Looking back up to the top of the wall, she could see floor joists sitting on top of the cinder blocks. A possible way out! Holding that thought in her mind, she was finally able to focus and completely separate herself from what was going on; her awareness was entirely on the darkened spaces between the joists and nothing else.

Emily's vision flashed again.

The man had left, and she was alone. She could see that there were some old empty crates along the wall. She thought that if she could stack them high enough, she could reach the top of the wall and peer into the darkened spaces between.

She stacked the crates up the wall and stepped onto them so that she could look between the joists. A crawl space!

She could see that the joists ran parallel with the direction she needed to pull herself to escape. With the thrill of the discovery still rushing through her body, Emily pulled herself into the opening and gradually repositioned herself until she was lying on her back; then she began to slowly drag herself forward, using the occasional crossbeam to grab hold of and pull herself along the channel between the two larger joists. As she dragged herself along, she could smell the combination of dry dirt and wood, but that soon gave way to a draft of air, raising goose bumps over her sweaty skin. She was close to an opening. She cricked her neck so that she could see what was ahead of her. It was still nighttime.

She reached her arms up past her head and could feel a screen blocking her path. She pushed against it, and the rusty metal gave way, and she could feel the outside of the house. With one last pull, she scooted herself out of the space enough that she could sit up and turn herself back over onto her front and crawl along the grass. She stayed in that position for just a moment, enough to catch her breath. Looking up, she surveyed her surroundings. This house looked familiar from the outside. The next house over was nearly thirty yards away. If she could carefully and quietly make her way along the side of the building, she thought, maybe she could better assess her surroundings. As she crept along the wall to the front corner of the house, she looked over to the house across the way, just to the left from this one. It was directly across the street from where she now stood. If she could make a run for it, she could get to that house and get help. As her eyes began to adjust, she could see, across the way, a tree swing in the front of the yard, just like the one her dad put up for her in her own front yard. Then she could see the familiar floral-patterned curtains in the window. At that moment, she knew exactly where she was, and she began to run.

23

Revelations

Emily awoke in the dark. For a moment, she forgot that she was safe in Chloe's bed. She sat up and leaned back against the headboard, her heart racing. She began to feel a chill come over her. Her clothing was damp with sweat. For the first time since it had happened, she understood what she had protected herself from ever since she was a child.

As her eyes adjusted to the dark, she could see Alex lying in the bed next to her. He was asleep. What time was it, she wondered. Then she realized, her phone was somewhere back at the apartment.

"Fuck!" Emily whispered aloud.

She could see, through Chloe's window, that it was night. Now she wasn't even sure what day it was. Ever so quietly, she attempted to slide herself to the edge of the bed, being careful not to wake Alex.

"You okay, babe?" mumbled Alex in a groggy tone, his eyes

still shut.

"Sorry, I didn't mean to wake you," she whispered.

Alex turned onto his side and took Emily's hand in his.

"How are you feeling, Em?" he asked, softly. "I thought I heard you in here, calling out earlier, so I came in here to check on you. By the time I'd gotten in here, you were fast asleep again, and I figured you'd had a bad dream. I didn't want to wake you or anything, and I must have been pretty tired myself from the drive here, so I laid down with you."

Emily turned toward Alex and rubbed his arm with her other hand.

"Where's Chloe?" Emily whispered.

"She fell asleep on the couch."

"Thanks for making the drive up here. It's been a really challenging couple of days. I'm not sure how much Chloe told you, but—."

Alex cut in, not wanting her to have to relive it all again, "She told me enough."

"Did she show—"

"She showed me everything she had on her phone, and I'm just glad I'm here now." Alex shifted himself onto his back and stared at the ceiling, "I can't even begin to explain what I saw in those videos, but it was terrifying. I honestly don't know how you've been able to go back to that place day in and day out."

The pair laid together in silence, both staring up at the ceiling. In the calm of this moment, lying next to Alex, Emily began trying to piece her nightmarish visions together in her head. It was all still too much. She needed more time to process what had happened to her in that basement before she could talk about it. Her mind, instead, drifted to Louise.

Emily wondered how Louise's molestation might have played a part in her spirit making itself known. Surely, Emily's own past was seeping into the existing energy swirling around her apartment; no question, Madeleine Bloom had sensed the same.

"What are you thinking about? I know you can get stuck in your head. Do you want to talk about it?" asked Alex.

"I'm just thinking about everything that had happened to me inside that apartment," Emily answered. "You know, everything I've talked to you about on the phone the last few weeks; Madeleine's observations, the story that Hazel told me about Louise's abuse, and then I haven't even told you this yet, but when Chloe and I were at Hazel's apartment, she showed me a box that belonged to Louise. It had a bunch of things inside, including some pictures. I picked up a picture of this man who Hazel told us was named Mr. Flowers and had an *instant*, visceral response. I mean, I could *hear his voice* as soon as I saw that picture."

"What do you think it all means?"

"I don't know yet," said Emily, trying to juggle each piece of this mental puzzle. "The sounds, those voices, the pungent cigar smell, and the smoke that came out of the center of the room — all of it was related to what had happened to Louise. It's as if that apartment is its own negative energy generator, literally swirling together everything that Louise had tormented herself with over her entire lifetime."

"Do you mean to suggest that all of it, including the damage I saw on Chloe's phone, is Louise?" Alex interjected, still a little confused.

"I'm beginning to suspect that Louise herself may have conjured all the negative energy that's now manifesting throughout my apartment. I can only imagine how much horrible psychic energy a person could create, tormenting themselves, day after day, with self-defeating thoughts like that."

Emily began to think to herself how much her own memories, including those she had suppressed, had harmed her throughout her life. She wasn't yet ready to open up to Alex, or anyone for that matter, about the trauma she now realized she, too, had suffered. But everything about her withdrawn demeanor made more sense now. Emily's mind had protected her to some extent; her subconscious had locked everything up, but Emily could still feel the anguish, sadness, and despair of that incident — all byproducts of her trauma. She'd become distant with friends and family, and that provided another layer of protection, but it also distanced her from anybody who might help her to heal.

"Em? Are you still there?" Alex asked, with a yawn.

"I'm here…. I'm still just thinking."

"I'm really tired. I'm sorry. I want to know more, but I can't stay awake. Would you mind if we pick this back up in the morning?"

"Yeah, go to sleep, sweetie," Emily said softly. "Love you."

Alex murmured something that sounded like 'love you, too' back to Emily as he drifted off to sleep again.

Emily continued to think more about Louise's agony.

Suffering a trauma at such a young age, as Louise did, Emily surmised, would undoubtedly have a major effect on her behavior from that point forward.

Whereas her own coping mechanism came in the form of isolating herself from the outside world, Louise's emotional circuits were tripped in a different way. It was possible that's why she developed into someone so uniquely sexualized —

and why she had so many self-destructive relationships.

Maybe that was why, until she herself came to live in that apartment, no one else reported seeing anything in the building or had any paranormal encounters in the apartment at all. Emily grew increasingly certain that Louise had been doing her best to assist Emily, a kindred spirit, in identifying the bad energy haunting the place.

24

The Scene of the Crime

Even in the light of a new day, Emily was hesitant to face whatever waited for them within her apartment, but she was also wary of running into her neighbors, who she was sure were going to be coming for her with pitchforks and torches over the noise that must have occurred in that apartment while they were gone. Still, she knew she should at least put a note on the door, something like: 'Pardon the dust – renovations in progress.' She also, at the very least, wanted to see if she could retrieve her cellphone.

For their part, Alex and Chloe were still curious to return to the space once more. Chloe knew the dangers of the apartment firsthand, but now that Alex had viewed the video footage captured the previous day, he wanted to see the damage for himself, and Chloe figured there was strength in numbers.

Emily took the lead as they walked up to the door leading into the lobby from the laundry room in the garage. As they entered the lobby, they could see that someone was coming down in the elevator. They waited patiently for the numbers to move from six, to five, to four...until the elevator finally reached the ground floor and the doors swung open. A young couple stepped out of the elevator and greeted Emily and her companions on their way out. Emily smiled at them, exchanged the normal pleasantries, and introduced Alex and Chloe, not noticing the other person in the elevator.

"Well, hello, Miss Pierson," said a chipper voice from inside the elevator.

Emily glanced back and realized it was Richard, her landlord.

"Emily, allow me to introduce you to your new neighbors," he said, motioning to the young couple beside him. "This is Leonard and Alison Bettencourt."

The young man reached out to shake Emily's hand.

"Call me Leo."

"I'm Ally," the young woman said, smiling.

"What floor are you on?" asked Emily.

"Oh, they're actually moving in on your floor," replied the landlord. "In fact, you two share a wall."

"Oh, wow," said Emily. "So, you're literally my new next-door neighbors?"

"Yeah, I guess so," said Ally.

"Say, Emily," said the landlord. "I actually thought you were home."

"Oh?"

"Yeah, I could have sworn I heard you next door when we were just upstairs."

Emily glanced over at Chloe and Alex.

"Oh, my friend Tammy...she's waiting for us upstairs," said Emily, stepping quickly into the elevator. "We don't want to keep her waiting."

Her landlord and her new neighbors said their goodbyes, and Chloe and Alex joined Emily in the elevator.

On the third floor, Emily, Alex, and Chloe stood side by side, gazing down the hall to Emily's door.

"Who's gonna go in first?" Emily asked.

"Not it," said Chloe, her standard response.

Emily turned to Chloe and shook her head, then made a move toward the door. Alex took her arm to stop her.

"I can go in first—" Alex said.

"It's fine; it is *my* home."

Emily began walking down the corridor, taking out her key to unlock the door, her friends close behind. Emily fully expected to see even more upheaval if the landlord had heard noises in the apartment. She pushed on the door. It swung open slowly in an arc, disturbing the dust motes floating in the air, to slam against the wall. They all jumped.

As the three of them peered into the room from the hallway, Emily and Chloe noticed that the dining room table had been moved again. It was now lying upside down, and the dining chairs looked as though they'd been hurled across the room. Emily thought to herself that she probably needed to talk to Richard, the landlord, about any noise complaints from her neighbors. After all, the neighbor below her tended to react to minor things, like walking "too aggressively."

Emily entered the apartment, furtively, the others two inches behind her, flanking her like battle weary soldiers. Emily gingerly stepped over some debris to get back into her bedroom. Her clothing was strewn about the room, and the bedsheets were still piled up at the foot of the bedframe, but the mattress had been pulled up off the bed and was now leaning against the window, blocking anyone's view into the apartment from the outside.

"Jesus" Alex said, right behind Emily. He moved passed her over toward the window and the mattress that was blocking it.

"I wouldn't bother with that," Emily said, clutching Alex's arm, "This isn't over. We'll just need to fix it again later."

Alex moved back out of the bedroom and into the main room, still wanting to make himself useful, somehow.

As Emily surveyed her bedroom, looking for her phone, a disembodied voice spoke into her ear.

"You don't belong here!" it said in a gravelly whisper.

"Did you guys hear that?" Emily called out to her companions in the other room.

"No, Em," said Alex. Chloe and Alex grabbed sides of the couch, that was leaning against the wall, to lower it back into place. "What did you hear?"

"The voice said, 'You don't belong here.'"

Having put the couch back into place, Alex and Chloe moved back into the bedroom to see if they could hear anything.

"You don't belong here!" the voice repeated.

"What the fuck was that?" asked Chloe.

"It's him," said Emily, her voice growing cold. "It's Mr. Flowers."

"Let's get out of here," Alex said, quickly backing out of the apartment. "Come on!" he yelled to the two women.

"But my phone!" Emily whined.

"Fuck your phone!" Chloe responded. "I'll buy you a new one. Why do we keep coming back here?" she muttered to herself as they exited the apartment.

Standing in the hall, Emily grabbed the door and tried to pull it shut. It resisted until Alex grabbed Emily's wrist. Together, they were able to close and lock the door. Staring at the door, they could see shadows moving under the door frame, like someone was inside, pacing in front of the door. They backed away slowly, keeping an eye on the door as they walked backward towards the elevator. Mercifully, the elevator doors opened with a cheerful ding just as they arrived.

"We shouldn't come back here alone," said Alex.

"Obvi, duh," said Chloe. "I'll call Madeline."

25

Digging deeper

Back at Chloe's apartment, Chloe called Madeleine Bloom. She informed her that they had recorded evidence of paranormal activity in the apartment and hoped that she could join them to provide more help. Madeleine said she could come over within the hour.

"Guys, I need to talk to you," Emily said softly.

"Is this about the voice we heard in your apartment?" Chloe asked.

"Yeah, but there's more…a lot more."

They each chose an oversized piece of furniture to settle into, and Emily took a moment, sitting quietly, before starting to talk. Emily had decided that speaking with Alex and Chloe about what had happened to her on that hot summer night twenty years ago might help her to clarify her own memories of the experience.

"First off, you guys both know about the weird dreams I've been having," Emily began. "I couldn't make sense of them, so I'd only mentioned the few that I started to realize a connection to, the ones that I'm sure were about Louise, for instance."

"But I've had some dreams more recently that are truly terrifying. I couldn't even find the will to tell either of you about them. They were too disturbing — and confusing." Emily scooted herself forward a bit in her chair. She started to ring her hands, swaying back and forth as she struggled to find the best way to broach the subject at hand.

"I don't know of any other way to say this except to just come out with it."

Alex turned to glance at Chloe who returned his look of concern.

"I was kidnapped outside a corner store," Emily began, struggling at first.

Alex and Chloe gasped.

"It was a long time ago; I was twelve when it happened. I'd ridden my bike there to get candy and a soda. I'd been there hundreds of times before, and it was near my house, so my parents were never worried about my safety. Why should they? Nothing bad ever went down in Cherryvale.

"Because the man who kidnapped me wore a mask, I never saw his face. He blindfolded me and tied my hands together. Man, it was quick. So quick. I'd seen ranch hands, cowboys, you know, like the ones you see at the rodeo when they rope the calves...

"He had a familiar odor, but I couldn't identify it at the time. I was much too frightened to speak. I honestly thought he'd kill me if I uttered a sound. The guy drove for what seemed like hours until he came to a stop.

"I could hear him open his door and exit the car. And I could hear his boots on the gravel as he got nearer to my side of the car. When the door opened, I was grabbed and carried away.

Through a small gap in the blindfold, I could see these tall reeds bending in the breeze on either side of the path."

Emily raised her hands up, moving them from side to side in a waving motion.

As she continued, Emily struggled to explain to her closest friend and boyfriend what happened next. She started to tear up as she recounted what this man had done to her.

"I could hear him unbuckle his belt. He was breathing heavily; it was disgusting. And then I could feel his whole weight on top of me. I tried to think about something else. Anything else; the scent of the dirt; I'd cut my lip at some point and I could taste the blood from that, and the gravel he'd put me on was excruciatingly hot, I'll never forget that.

"I pleaded with the guy to stop. I screamed, thinking someone might hear me. I cried out that I couldn't take the pain from the hot gravel... He ignored it all.

"That was the first time he raped me. When he was done, he grabbed me up and pushed me back inside the car, then pushed me off the seat and onto the floor under the dashboard.

"I just laid there, motionless. I didn't make a sound. To tell you the truth, I'd become desensitized to the possibility of what could happen next. And I think, at that point, I had resolved that I was going to die that night.

"After what felt like an hour or more, I noticed the car slowing and then pulling onto another road. I could hear crickets chirping and wondered whether my folks might be concerned about me. For a brief second, I worried they'd be mad at me for being out so late, but by this point, I'd lost all concept of time.

"He tossed me over his shoulder, walked into a house, and shrugged me off his back onto the floor. He opened another door, grabbed my feet, and dragged me down some stairs into a cellar. Before freeing my hands, the man leaned in close and slowly pulled down my blindfold. I kept my eyes closed, but I could feel his hot breath against my face.... And then I heard that voice.

"'You're really beautiful,' he said to me, softly. Then he grabbed my face and growled, 'you'd better keep those pouty little lips shut, or you'll end up dead in the basement.'

"I heard him go up some stairs and then I heard the door slam shut. I remember lying there frozen for a long time. I thought that if I moved, if I made any noise, he would come back down. But eventually I could hear him stomping around on the floor above me, and then I heard his car start, so I knew I was alone.

As Emily continued to tell her story, both Chloe and Alex sat transfixed. Tears streamed down Chloe's face as she listened to Emily.

Emily continued again.

"I don't really know how much time had passed, but I started to look around. I couldn't see too much. My eyes were still adjusting. The basement I was in had one light and it was dim, like it was on the verge of going out. I started to glance around the space, and that's when I saw a weird bundle of plastic in the corner. It was the corpse of another girl. Even though she was covered in plastic, I could see her face. She looked pale, I think she had been strangled, but I don't know. She was so still, and her mouth was wide open, like she died screaming or gasping for breath. It was so horrifying. I realized that I recognized her from the neighborhood. I was two or three years older than she was, but I knew her because we'd played together when we were younger.

"All of this, everything I've told you both, this is the first time I've told anyone. And it wasn't because I tried to keep it all a secret. It's because I couldn't remember any of it. I literally blocked it out. And then I moved into that apartment. 3-0-7- North-fucking-Goodman Street. I started having these dreams. Nightmares. I didn't understand what they were. Over time, I started trying to piece together the bits and pieces that were coming back to me.

"But then I had a nightmare that was worse than all the rest. I saw what that fucking psycho had done to her. That's when I realized what he'd planned for me if I hadn't found a way out of that cellar. In my dream, I saw that he had dug a deep hole out in a corn field where he was sure no one would ever find her."

Emily paused for a moment. In her mind's eye, she could now almost picture the scene from above, and she tried her best to remain detached so that she could get her thoughts out.

"He buried Izzy in the middle of that corn field. He waited until dark, then carried her body, and a shovel, deep inside the field where he knew no one would be able to see what he was doing while he dug that hole, using the tall stocks as cover."

"That girl," Chloe said, a look of deep thought pouring over her face, "you said her name was Izzy? Do you remember her last name?"

"Her name was Izzy Santos."

"Izzy?" Chloe asked, "as in Elizabeth?

"Yeah, why?

"Was her name Elizabeth *Rose* Santos?"

"How do *you* know that?" Alex uttered, confused. Emily could see how rattled he was. "Emily, I'm so, so sorry. I can't imagine what that was like for you."

"I know that name because they mentioned it on the news feed," Chloe said. "They reported the remains of another child, *Elizabeth Rose Santos,* that had been found somewhere around Cherryvale. That's your hometown; I thought you heard the same thing when we were all watching it in the bullpen. They linked her remains to a serial killer, called the Scarecrow Killer."

Emily felt a chill come over her. She and Izzy were victims of a serial killer?

26

A Way Forward

Madeleine was running late, so Alex decided to make lunch, not knowing when they would have another opportunity to eat. Sitting around, they continued to mull through all the recent events and revelations. Invariably, the conversation came back around to Louise.

"I wonder whether the man who molested Louise had managed to somehow attach himself to her after he died," Emily pondered. "Louise may have inadvertently 'invited' this guy's spirit into that space by obsessing over what happened to her all those years ago. Maybe this thing gained power every time Louise, more or less, brought him back to life, in her thoughts without even realizing it."

Emily realized, there was another possibility.

"Do you think it's possible for a location to just absorb the most powerful feelings of people who inhabit it?" Emily asked Chloe and Alex.

"Could Louise have conjured up this evil entity, like literally, out of thin air?" Chloe asked.

"If that's the case, that... thing... showed a shocking amount of strength," answered Alex.

"You see that kind of stuff happen in horror movies, but it always seems so fake." Chloe added, "This legit happened to you, Em! We all saw it!"

"If all of that paranormal activity has been confined to my apartment," Emily said, beginning to piece elements together, "I can think of only one more possibility that would explain why it was able to chase you and me down the hall—"

"It literally tried to force itself into Hazel's apartment when we got over *there*" Chloe interjected.

"I have to assume Mr. Flowers was long dead when Louise moved into that apartment." Emily continued, growing more intense, "I really do think that Louise somehow unwittingly created the thing that's in the apartment now!"

"How is that possible, Em?" Alex asked.

"I think she somehow conjured it—"

"Conjured it how?" Alex, pushed again, emphatically.

"From all of the terrifying memories she must have kept obsessing over, for years!" Emily pushed back at Alex, now with more conviction, "It's like she *caused* him to manifest — out of thin air — long after he'd already been dead and buried!"

"Maybe that would explain why it was trapped?" Chloe wondered, aloud.

Chloe may have stumbled onto an important distinction. As terrifying as it now seemed, Emily now wondered if the entity that chased her and Chloe wasn't the same entity at all. Emily trained her gaze down at the floor.

"Once Louise had died in that apartment," Emily continued,

deep into her thoughts, "the energy would've had nowhere else to go, right? Without Louise there anymore to feed it with negative energy, nothing else could bring it back to life, so it laid dormant all this time."

"That's right," acknowledged Chloe.

"Hazel told us that nobody had reported any sort of paranormal anything — for all these years — until I moved in."

"Uh huh..." Chloe nodded.

"So, what does that mean?" Emily said, confused.

The trio sat together, silently thinking to themselves. The theory that Emily thought she'd started to pull together was now gone.

"The drawing!" shouted Chloe, excitedly, waving her hands in front of Emily. "That creepy-as-fuck drawing those kids drew the night of your housewarming; there was a third thing in that drawing!"

Emily stared at Chloe as her friend continued to explain.

"Louise was one of them," Chloe continued, "and then there was the guy they drew wearing overalls — just like Mr. Flowers wore — in that photo you found in Louise's box that Hazel showed us..."

Emily was tracking along with Chloe now, "But that other thing — that tall, black slender-man-looking thing they drew by the closet —"

"Exactly!" Chloe shouted, "That's something totally new to all of this. I have no clue what it is or where it came from, but maybe that thing isn't confined to just your apartment... but why? ...how?"

Chloe slumped back into the couch, unable to take her thought further. Without realizing it, Chloe had given her friend the last piece of the puzzle.

Emily could finally stitch the pieces together for herself.

She knew who the black figure was in the drawing. And now she knew that it was this figure that had been terrorizing her in some of her more recent nightmares regarding the basement — and the crawl space. This entity was combining its energy with all the other negative energy swirling about that space. This thing was something unrelated to Louise, and to Louise's monster.

Emily now had to come to terms with the fact that this was an entity that she herself had brought into the space. She had conjured something of her own making, much the same way that Louise had done over so many years before in the spirit of Mr. Flowers. Because Emily could move freely about the building, she began to fear that this third entity had the power to do the same, unlike Mr. Flowers, who she speculated was still trapped.

* * *

When Madeleine Bloom arrived at Chloe's apartment, she was met with a flurry of questions from the group.

"Emily, Chloe, I'm so appreciative that you felt confident enough in me to call me back," Madeleine began. "I've been wondering what's been going on since we last talked."

Chloe spoke up first.

"Madeleine, I really do owe you an apology." Chloe said.

"Please, don't give it another thought."

"Madeleine, I was really rude to you. I didn't like how I left things with you," said Chloe, taking Madeleine's hand in hers, "I was just—"

"You were worried for your friend," Madeleine interjected.

"To tell you the truth, you were right to take me to task. I told you that there was a lot of scary stuff going on in that apartment, and then I just sort of left you both to somehow deal with it... all by yourselves."

Chloe nodded, sympathetically as Madeleine continued, "If anything, I owe you an apology. I'm hoping to correct all of that with you now, though."

Chloe, still holding Madeleine's hand, motioned her to sit down on her couch, nearest Emily.

Finally, Alex moved himself forward on the couch and reach over to shake Madeleine's hand.

"Hello, Mrs. Bloom," Alex said, enthusiastically. "I'm Alex."

"He's my boyfriend," Emily explained, briefly rubbing her hand across Alex's back.

"It's a pleasure to meet you, Alex," Madeleine began, her eyebrows beginning to furrow. "So tell me, Alex, are you up to speed with everything these lovely ladies and I talked about on my first visit?"

"Oh yeah, absolutely. I live in New York City, but Em and Chloe both have been keeping me updated on everything that's been going on, including the initial visit you made to Em's apartment."

Emily was anxious to update Madeleine further on some of her latest revelations.

"Madeleine, I've been having dreams over the last several months," Emily said, eager to get started. "If I'm being completely honest, they sort of began at roughly the same time that I moved into that apartment."

"Chloe mentioned, over the phone to me, that the activity in your apartment has gotten much worse."

"It has, yes, and I think these dreams are the connection."

"I'm not sure I follow," said Madeleine.

"I think the dreams I've been having are Louise's way of communicating with me. Does that make sense?"

"Oh, *that* absolutely makes sense. It's one of the easiest ways for the departed to make contact with us. It takes much less energy for them to manifest inside our dreams."

"Some of the dreams have been more disturbing than others. Often, visions will flash at me — horrifying images — and they're sometimes enough to wake me up in the middle of the night."

"Well what sort of things are you seeing in these… nightmares?"

"Well, I was actually talking with Chloe and Alex about them before you arrived. I think I've finally managed to piece some of them together to the point that we have a working hypothesis."

"Well, have at it," said Madeleine, encouraged to see that they were working constructively. "Please tell me what you've got." Madeleine shifted back into the couch in preparation for what she might hear next. "If I get any sort of confirmation from my spirit guides, I will let you know."

"Well, we think there are three distinct spirits in the apartment," began Emily. "One of them is obviously Louise Brooks. The other one, that one man you described as wearing overalls, we think that might be a man from Louise's past. I've been doing a lot more research on Louise since we last spoke, and it turns out, she had a secret in her past that I think she carried with her throughout her entire life."

Madeleine sat attentively as she listened to Emily. "In my experience," Madeleine interjected, "Secrets are never good to hold onto. They can fester, and they can emit a sort of negative energy that I believe these other entities can tap into."

"That's exactly what I think has happened in my case," Emily answered before posing another question to Madeleine. "Do you think it's possible for a person to create an entity?"

"How do you mean, dear?"

"Like...out of thin air?"

"Well, yes dear, I suppose that *is* possible. Everything we're talking about, the stuff in your apartment, hell..., ghosts in general, it's all just energy. I'm sure you've heard it said that inanimate objects can soak up the energy from a particularly traumatic event, say a shooting, for instance, or a terrible fight. If you get enough of that — in one particular space — all of that negative energy can build up. For those of us, like myself..., and I think possibly yourself, who are sensitive..., we can pick up on that bad energy."

"But can a living person create an entity... all on their own?"

"Yes, they can. In fact, there have been experiments done, that I've heard about, where paranormal researchers have gone to a 'haunted' location, one that has stories connected to it that have been passed along from person to person over the years. Perhaps the story is about the ghost of a young boy who was killed in a terrible fire; rubber balls and other toys are laid out all over the floor, throughout the location, and people are encouraged to interact with the ghost of that little boy. Well, as it turns out, researchers have conducted experiments where they will introduce a different story into such a space; they will implant a completely innocuous thought into those who visit the space. They might say, for instance, that the person who lived in the house was famous for having saved someone from drowning and that they lived a long and harmonious life. Before long, people will report that the negative energy they once felt in the space has disappeared."

"You mean to say they're actually able to change the creepy vibe of the place, just by giving the house a non-threatening story?" Chloe asked, completely enthralled by what Madeleine was suggesting. "Sort of like giving the place a re-set?"

"That's what I'm saying," Madeleine answered.

Emily needed more clarification. "So it might be possible, then, for Louise, who lived in that space for such a long time, and who held on to all that negative stuff from her past, to implant that space with this entity that she simply just conjured for herself — with just her thoughts?"

"I think it's possible, yes," said Madeleine.

"So do we need any special gear? Holy water?" asked Chloe. "Do we need to learn a chant or something?"

Madeleine smiled. "I think you've been watching too many movies. All we need is to go together, remain strong, and confront this negative entity with…"

"An alternate story?" interjected Emily.

"Yes, perhaps. But I think it will be important to go, armed with facts. You mentioned you'd been doing research on Louise, and that you'd come to understand what secret she may have been carrying with her while she was alive?"

"I think it was the fact that she'd been molested at about the age of nine; it was a handyman who'd done work for several of the families in the neighborhood. She called him 'Mr. Flowers.'"

"We even saw a picture of him," Chloe added. "Did we bring that box back here with us, Em?"

Emily nodded at Chloe, then glanced back at Madeleine. "Would you like to see it?"

"Yes, please. Could I hold it?"

Emily went into the other room and returned with the box of items she'd received from Hazel, then sat down next to Madeleine and presented her with the photo of the man in overalls. Madeleine took the photo into her hand and closed her eyes.

"May I also hold the box please?" Madeleine asked, her eyes still shut tight.

Emily extended the box to Madeleine. "It's right here."

Madeleine took it into her hands and leaned her head back, as if in a trance.

"I believe your theory is correct, my dear."

"Really?"

"Yes. Now be sure to bring all this back to the apartment with you," Madeleine said, placing the box onto the table in front of them, then tapping on it. "I'm assuming you want me to go back there with you?"

"Yes, Ma'am." Emily replied softly.

"Now you said you've been piecing these ideas together to form your hypotheses," said Madeleine, turning her gaze back over to Emily, now with more intensity. "I'm sensing there's more you haven't told me."

Emily nodded.

"Did you ever resolve whatever the crawl space was about?"

Emily nodded again.

"...Because I must tell you," Madeleine continued, "sitting here next to you, I'm picking up on it again."

"That was the third part of all this that I think I've pieced together," Emily began. "First off, you were right about the crawl space when you brought it up to me the first time, when we talked outside my apartment building. At the time, I knew only that it was something from my own past, not Louise's. I

183

didn't want to get into it any further because it was something I hadn't come to terms with, myself, yet. I'd apparently blocked it from my mind completely, sort of as a coping mechanism, I guess, to get over the trauma of what happened to me."

Madeline leaned forward and placed her hand gently on Emily's shoulder, "My spirit guides are telling me that a big part of what's going on in that apartment, the really angry, volatile stuff, is this energy that *you've* been storing up… and putting out all around you."

"But how is that possible? The guy who did this to me is still alive!"

"All the more reason it's so strong."

Emily nodded in agreement. Everything Madeleine was telling her made sense to her now.

"Let's get down to brass tacks, shall we?" Madeleine began. "We're going to need to devise a strategy for getting rid of all that paranormal activity. It's become a lot angrier, and you can't just go in there, without a plan."

Emily, Chloe, and Alex sat quietly, watching Madeleine, who sat before them as though she were commanding the attention of a group of kids in front of a campfire.

"Emily," said Madeleine.

"Yes, ma'am?"

"In order to put an end to everything that's going on inside that apartment, you need to follow through."

"What do you mean?" asked Emily. "How?"

"You can't do any of this halfway. You've got to commit yourself entirely. You've got to drag all of this negative energy into the light of day. Only then will you be able to expel that evil spirit that's got you trapped, so to speak, that has Louise's spirit trapped — and finally, put Louise's spirit at peace and free her once and for all. I'll do my part in helping her to cross over, but you're going to have to do a lot of the heavy lifting since a lot of this energy is connected to you and *your* past."

"Do you really think we can all get rid of this entity in Em's apartment?" asked Alex, clearly needing more reassurance.

"Look, Louise's soul lacks the capacity to break away from her earthly bonds," Madeleine explained. "She's trapped here."

Madeleine hunched forward, "In life, she never realized what all her negative energy and self-sabotage were conjuring inside that apartment. She didn't know how to get help. Instead, she ruminated on her traumatic memories until all that evil was attracted by her immense pain and took up residence until you unwittingly moved into her apartment. You might have something in your past that may be feeding the same evil energy attracted to this place."

Alex squeezed Emily's shoulder, reassuringly.

"Louise can no longer clean up her own mess. She's dead, so we need do it for her." Madeleine turned her attention to Emily. "You, on the other hand, have a mess of your own. The good news is that you're still very much alive."

Emily smiled tentatively.

"Have you had to deal with something this intense before?" Chloe asked with an edge of worry.

"This isn't my first time dealing with something of this magnitude, but I must admit that it is rare. All I can say is that I think I can help you fix this, and I'll stay with all of you through the entire process. I did have a case several years ago where an entity was not immediately convinced to leave. It's not always enough when the person, or persons, connected to the entities fights back, but it helps to have a supportive group. Having me there along with Chloe and Alex to support you should be enough. In my experience, it always comes down to a battle of wills. I believe in you, and so do Alex and Chloe.

Emily looked down at her hands and sighed.

Gently lifting Emily's chin, Madeline continued, "You have the power to seize control *back* from the man who took so much away from *you*, Emily," her eyes locking on Emily's. "We have a chance to rid you and the apartment of all evil energy and set Louise free once and for all. It's time to clean house!"

There was only one thing left to do; face the paranormal infestation head on.

27

Pandora's Box

By the time they returned to Emily's apartment, it was almost 7:00 p.m. The street in front of Emily's building was empty. The fallen snow created a sense of stillness. Christmas lights twinkled from several windows in the building.

As Emily got out of her car, she looked up at the building that had been her home — and her torment — for the past few months and felt confident and ready to take on any challenge. She held out her hand to Alex in a gesture of solidarity. Alex took her hand and smiled. Chloe glanced at the two of them and grinned.

Madeleine stepped out of the car.

Chloe ushered them all into a circle. "So, what's the game plan? Are we really ready for this? How do we help you, Madeline?"

Madeline, sounding confident, said, "On the way over here, I was connecting with my spirit guides, preparing myself mentally, for whatever might confront us in there. Just follow my lead."

She glanced up at the third-floor window and started to turn back toward Emily, when her attention was drawn back to the window. Without turning her head, she said, "I sense a lot more hostile energy than the last time I was here." Dragging her eyes from the window, she turned to Emily. "The evil must have sensed you the minute we arrived."

As they all entered the lobby, the lights grew dim for a few moments before regaining their full strength.

They began to enter the elevator when Madeleine stopped everyone.

"Hey, y'all," she said. "Maybe we should take the stairs this one time."

Chloe and Alex looked at each other, then glanced at Emily, who nodded to Madeleine in agreement.

They walked in single file with Emily leading the way as they walked down the corridor to the stairwell in the back of the building. At the foot of the stairs, Emily put out her hand, motioning everyone to stop.

"I'm feeling a sense that something doesn't want us to go any further."

She turned to Madeline. "Can you feel it?"

Just then, the lights in the staircase went out, and they could all hear a door shaking and rattling above them.

"Everyone, hold onto the railing and stay close." Emily warned, "whatever it is that I'm feeling wants to stop us, maybe even by trying to harm us physically."

Chloe muttered, "you owe me a big fucking Christmas gift" before pulling out her cellphone and switching on the flashlight.

"Everything's gonna be just fine, Chloe," Emily assured her. "It's trying to scare us, but we're not going to let it, are we?"

Chloe shook her head, unconvincingly, as they continued up the stairs to the third-floor landing, the menacing sound of the door growing louder.

In the glare of the cell phone flashlight, they could all see the doorknob twisting back and forth as they approached. Emily seized the doorknob and flung the door open. They stepped into the hallway and slowly crept towards Emily's apartment. As they approached the door to Emily's apartment, the screws holding the knob in place began to unscrew. They watched, frozen in shock, as the screws fell, one by one, to the hallway floor. Drawing closer, they jumped back as the knob slid out of the door frame and tumbled to the floor.

Madeline moved to stand in front of them and said, "let me go in first. Alex, do you think you can kick open the door for me?"

Alex poked at the door with his foot, checking to see if the door was still fastened even though the doorknob had fallen out. Feeling resistance, he backed up a bit, and kicked the door, trying to strike with the ball of his foot, imagining his foot going through the door. It slammed open.

They all lined up behind Madeline and gingerly followed her inside as she surveyed the space. This was her first time seeing the apartment in this condition, with everything strewn about. They slowly, but cautiously, walked around, eventually ending up in the bedroom.

A disembodied voice snarled at them as they entered Emily's bedroom, *"You don't belong here...."*

Emily's demeanor shifted. She had a look of defiance now as she side-stepped her way ahead of the group and entered her bedroom.

"I don't belong here?" Emily shouted into the room. "NO... YOU don't belong here, you worthless piece of shit!"

Alex turned his attention to the closet door, which had begun swinging wildly back and forth, slamming against the door frame like a window shutter in a storm.

"IS THAT ALL YOU CAN DO?" Emily shouted, planting both of her feet firmly.

"THIS IS MY HOME!" Emily screamed; her fists clenched. "YOU HAVE NO RIGHT TO BE HERE!"

"Yes, keep going!" said Madeline.

As Emily scanned the room once again, she adjusted herself so that she was facing away from her friends, who could only stare in awe. None of them was paying attention to the fact that the bedsheets, which had been flung into a heap on the floor, were starting to slither across the room toward Emily.

Alex noticed the bedsheets when one end curled around Emily's ankle. Before he could warn her, the cloth had tightened firmly around her leg. He rushed over and grabbed the sheet where it was attached to her leg. Emily screamed and tried to shake her leg while Alex futilely tugged. The sheet slithered up to her waist, immune to his efforts to free her, and yanked her to the ground.

Chloe glanced up just in time to see the mattress, which had been pushed up against the window, begin to teeter back the other way, straight for Emily, who was lying face down on the floor.

"Alex, LOOK OUT!" Chloe shouted, bolting across the room in hopes of catching the mattress before it landed on top of Emily.

As Alex and Madeline grabbed Emily and pulled her out

of harm's way, the mattress grazed Chloe across one of her shoulders as it tumbled to the floor. The sheet was now loose enough to pull away, and Alex rapidly unspooled it from her torso and leg.

They pulled Emily up, and then they all fled the bedroom; Alex slammed the bedroom door shut behind them.

"Well, Emily, you stood your ground nicely, but it's going to take another confrontation. Let's take a few deep breaths and then go in there again," Madeline advised.

As they stepped over lamps, chairs, and dishes that had been pulled from the cupboard, Chloe paused, eyebrows furrowed.

"Does anyone else smell that?" Chloe asked, befuddled. "It smells like burning chocolate."

"Yeah, I do," said Emily. "Maybe burned brownies?"

"Is that coming from another apartment?" said Alex.

Chloe rushed over and saw a pot on the stove. Its contents had boiled over, and the fudgy bits were catching fire in the flame underneath. She grabbed an oven mitt and took hold of the pot handle, pulling it to her and revealing a now charred mess inside. She waved her hands in front of her, fanning away the smoke rising from the encrusted pot, then lunged at the knob and turned off the burner.

"Alex, this pot was not on the stove the last time we were here, and I don't have any chocolate or brownie mix in the apartment" Emily said.

Alex turned to them and said, "Wait, didn't you tell us about a vision you had where Louise was lured by her molester with some chocolate or fudge?"

"Oh, my God, yes" Emily blurted.

Madeline added, "This ...could be the Mr. Flowers' entity trying to use past events to control the present. He knows that the memory of how Louise was first molested is part of the narrative that holds her in his power."

Before Emily could respond, the Christmas tree, still lying on its side, began to quiver, the lights blinking on and off rapidly. The ornaments started to explode one by one.

With her hands in fists by her sides, Emily screamed, "GET THE FUCK OUT OF MY APARTMENT! And keep your hands off my Christmas tree, you rapey little fuck."

The tree was silenced, the lights turned off, and the only sound in the apartment was one ornament slowly rocking on the floor.

Madeleine stood in the corner, feet planted; raising her hands to her temples, she tried to connect with the spirit world.

"Emily," Madeleine said softly. "This thing has a strong grip on the space. It's definitely connected to Louise's spirit. Given that it's been here ever since she died, I'm guessing it's been able to leverage its anonymity for a very long time. It's probably been storing up more and more energy with every new tenant who's lived in this space, before you, feeding on every negative emotion it could. But I'm also getting a strong sense that this thing is aware that you're the first person to live in this apartment who's developed a connection with Louise's spirit. It's also very much aware that you've done your homework when it comes to Louise — and it understands that you know exactly who he was in life. This would be the time for you to speak directly to the man who tormented Louise's memories for all those years."

Madeleine's suggestion wasn't lost on Emily, who understood that Louise's tormentor, who was presenting such a powerful display in this moment, was, in reality, nothing more than a worthless nobody that preyed on defenseless little girls.

She agreed with Madeleine that exposing him, in a way that nobody had ever done before, might actually force him out, once and for all.

"You see yourself as all-powerful," Emily began, building up her strength. "But I know exactly who you are!"

The tree lights began to flicker again, the curtains undulated as if by an invisible breeze, and the broken furniture pieces clattered against the floor.

"In life, you were EDWIN G. FLOWERS!" Emily shouted.

The framed picture of Louise Brooks was ripped off the wall by invisible hands and flung across the room, shattering at Emily's feet.

"You were a FUCKING PEDOFILE!" Emily yelled. "Louise isn't here anymore for you to torment!"

In that instant, Emily was lifted off the ground. She flailed her arms about, trying to keep herself righted. Before she could react any further, she was hurled into the wall, where she dropped to the floor, unconscious.

Alex dashed over to Emily and tried to pick her up. Her form was as limp as a doll. Realizing that it was safer to leave her in one spot, he checked her pulse and quickly checked her over for any blood or obvious injury.

Alex screamed, "We have to get her out of here!"

"I'm okay, Alex!" said Emily, regaining consciousness.

Madeline moved over to Emily and placed herself between Emily and the rest of the room as if to create a sort of psychic shield. "She just needs to catch her breath, but she's okay. It's imperative that she keeps up her attack in order to drive the negative energy from this place entirely!"

Emily began to move. She gave Alex a reassuring look that let him know she was alright and ready to continue. Alex helped her to her feet as Emily began, once again, addressing the room.

"I demand that you, Edwin G. Flowers, leave!" Emily exclaimed, stopping briefly before continuing, "You are not welcome here! This is my home! Louise conjured you…but she's not here anymore. We're going to see to it that her soul is finally free, and you will never again be able to hold her captive!"

Madeleine, Chloe and Alex stood beside her as she continued.

"You can't hide anymore, like you did when you were alive," Emily said. "I know everything about you, and soon, everyone else will, too. I'll tell your descendants what a piece of shit you were, and I'll make sure the cemetery where you're buried knows exactly who's buried there!"

A resonant rumble emanated from the room; Alex extended his hands to hold Emily's back to prevent her from falling as the floor began to quake.

A mass of dark plasma appeared above them and began to grow tendrils, swirling around the room, until fingers of it filled the ceiling space.

Undaunted, Emily continued, "You decided to prey on young girls because they couldn't fight back. You ruined so many young lives. You screwed up Louise, but she wasn't the only one. She was just the one who took you to the grave with her. Your time here is done."

In that moment, Emily looked up to see the swirling energy begin to disperse.

"Just leave!" Emily shouted with all her strength. "LEAVE!"

Madeline directed everyone to join Emily in banishing the entity.

Alex, Chloe, Madeline, and Emily all shouted "LEAVE!"

The room fell silent. They stood, waiting for the entity to respond. For several minutes, they waited, and nothing more happened.

"You did it, Emily, you got rid of him" Madeleine said. "I'm not feeling Mr. Flowers at all now."

Emily sighed and Alex wrapped her in a fierce embrace. Then, glancing around the room, Alex grabbed hold of the Christmas tree, righting it, and half-heartedly trying to straighten some of the strings of lights.

Chloe leaned against the wall and let out a deep sigh.

Emily turned to her friend. "You okay?"

"Not really. I'm glad Mr. Flowers is gone and all, but what about the other spider thing? I'm too tired to be scared of anything else at this point. I'll just go into your bedroom and pick some shit up. Call me if you need me. Hell, the rattling and screaming will tip me off," she ended sarcastically, then she made her way to the bedroom.

Alex took Emily's hand. "Are you okay?" he asked.

Emily shrugged. "Yeah," she said, leaning against him.

"You'll feel a lot better after you get some sleep."

"Yeah," she said.

"Do you need anything?"

Emily shook her head.

"Okay, I'm going to help Chloe."

"Thanks, Alex."

He left Emily and Madeleine alone in the room.

"I didn't want to say anything in front of Chloe, but she is right. You know we're not done here," Madeleine said gently.

Emily sighed and sat down on the edge of the couch. "Yes, I know."

Madeleine slowly walked around the room, carefully avoiding the clutter, the shattered remains of Emily's ornaments, the smokey haze from the burned fudge, wafting around her as she made her way to the window. She tilted her head forward, as though she were listening intently to something.

"Flowers is gone, but I can still feel the other... attachment." She paused, turning to face Emily. "It's so strange. I get the sense that it's here, but it's not. Does that mean anything to you?"

Emily nodded. "I think he's less here," Emily said, gesturing into the room. "It's here, in my head" Emily said, glancing back at Madeleine while tapping her temple. "But I think his energy will eventually fill this apartment too, just like Louise's tormentor did, if I let him."

"So, when I mentioned to you, before, about my sensing that insect-like thing seemed attached to you, somehow... that wasn't a surprise to you?"

"Oh, it was. It scared the shit out of me. I really didn't have a clue what it might be that could have attached itself to me. But a lot has happened since then... There was something terrible, from my own past, something that I'd apparently managed to completely block from my consciousness all this time. But I think that the dreams that I told you I've been having... I've come to believe that they were partly brought on by Louise. I think *she* was just as bothered by *my* past as she was her own. At any rate, I now think she was trying to bring my subconscious to the forefront so I could help myself — and her — in the process. Does that make sense?"

"It does," answered Madeleine. "It sounds like you had your own 'Mr. Flowers.'"

Over a lifetime, Emily had noticed how much more liberated

she felt the farther away from Cherryvale she got, and she became conscious of her tendency to shut down whenever she returned home.

Emily picked a Christmas tree ornament off the floor. As she held it in her hand, she thought about decorating the Christmas tree with Alex. Then it occurred to her that she always made sure she was otherwise busy during the holidays — too busy, at least, to travel back to Cherryvale. But it wasn't because of her relationship with her parents. Emily loved her parents, and she made it a point to catch up with them regularly by phone and video chat.

Emily's situation was different from Louise's in another critical way. The spirit that Louise had spawned was created out of the memories of a long-dead monster she'd held on to her entire life. In *Emily's* case, however, the perpetrator who raped her was still alive, and Emily had blocked him from her memory – as a survival reflex - until recently.

"I know who that shadow figure is" Emily said, as if in a trance.

"So, who is it?" asked Madeleine, curiously.

"It's the guy who raped me," Emily began. "And he was absolutely going to kill me if I hadn't found a way out of that basement."

Moreover, this was someone she knew before she was kidnapped. Yet again, Emily shared one more thing in common with Louise. They both knew their attackers. For Louise, it was the handyman who'd done odd jobs around the neighborhood.

Emily finally had the courage to say it out loud, "He was my neighbor across the street, Mr. Harris."

"I think I know what to do. And it won't be nearly as

hazardous to me or my stuff," she said, smiling weakly.

Emily sighed again, slumping on the couch, and rubbed her shoulder.

Then she took a deep breath.

She walked carefully through the broken items on the floor, then noticed her phone where it lay near the cupboards.

"I've been looking for this."

She ran her thumb along a crack across the screen of her phone.

"That son of a bitch cracked my screen." She gave a little laugh and slipped the phone into her back pocket.

Chloe and Alex walked back into the main room. Emily's smile had faded. She found the framed portrait of Louise lying face down on the floor, surrounded by broken glass. The frame was damaged but still intact. She removed a broken piece of glass that was still attached to the frame and placed it on the coffee table. Then, she placed the portrait, so it stood on the floor, leaning against the wall. She paused for a moment to look at Louise. She found the locket near the couch and hung it from the corner of the frame. She said nothing as she walked over to hug Chloe and then walked over to Alex and wrapped her arms around him. After a few moments, she pulled away and sobbed as she took her phone from her pocket. Then she took another breath and called the Cherryvale Police Department. When the dispatcher came on the line, Emily said, "Hello, my name is Emily Pierson. I was a victim of the Scarecrow Killer...."

28

Hunting the Scarecrow Killer

In the days after Emily first reached out to the local authorities, first in Cherryvale and later in Wichita, her unique perspective of the Scarecrow Killer proved crucial in helping Kansas authorities in their pursuit of the man they now knew to be Roger Harris.

The local authorities asked Emily if she could fly to Kansas to be interviewed and tell them everything she could. Emily was more than willing to make the trip back to Kansas this time, filled with a newfound empowerment and resolve to catch this serial killer.

Chloe saw all of this as a great story that the Rochester affiliate could cover.

"Local news team member's link to the Scarecrow Killer" Chloe suggested to Emily, waving her hands across the air, as if to suggest a marquee headline.

To say the station was enthusiastic would be an understatement. They covered the entire cost of Chloe and Emily's trip, which also included bringing Madeleine along for *her* own specific expertise. They were told to meet with the local affiliate in Wichita so that one of their local camera people could film whatever happened during their stay.

* * *

Having arrived in Wichita, the trio were picked up by the station manager and a camera person who'd driven to the airport in the WROC TV Channel 8 Van. Emily asked them if they could drive her directly to the police headquarters; she gave them the address the authorities had given her and told them she was anxious to get started.

It didn't take long to get to the destination. As Emily and her companions looked up, they could see the name on the building: Sedgwick County Sheriff.

As they approached the building's entrance, from the TV station's van, they were met by Sergeant McHenry who introduced himself as the person who headed up Wichita County's Crime Scene Investigations unit. He gave them a brief tour of the facility before sitting down with Emily to take her statement and have her corroborate any evidence they'd already collected so far, which, in this case, included mainly crime scene photos. For her part, Emily had seemed agitated and fidgety throughout the entire flight. Once they finally got to the CSI unit, she reviewed the evidence they'd collected, which didn't seem like much. Everything seemed to match up with what she remembered the killer had done with her, but she was surprised that this was all they had. Was there no DNA evidence? Something? Anything more that they might reveal to her? Emily seemed almost combative. It didn't help that Sergeant McHenry's first thought was to give the trio a tour. Emily couldn't help but feel that their time was being wasted — and she didn't fly to Kansas to get a VIP tour.

"Miss Pierson," the Sergeant began, "You've stated that you believe this Roger Harris to be the man who kidnapped you; is that correct?" He held up a mugshot photo of Roger Harris.

Emily was unaware that the man she'd spent so much time with during her childhood had a criminal record, at least enough of one that he'd had a mugshot taken.

"Yes, sir," Emily said, her tone serious but growing more exasperated. "I already told your officers about the basement and everything I knew about Mr. Harris."

"Yes, I'm aware of that, Miss Pierson," said the Sergeant. "We've had the local sheriff drive by the residence you told us about; the house is right next door to your parents' house, just as you said."

"Yes, it's 5270 West Main Street, in Cherryvale," Emily asserted, roughly. "Are you saying you haven't even walked up to the house and knocked on the door?"

"We have, Miss Pierson. It's just that Roger Harris no longer resides there; he's renting the place to someone, and it's taking some time for us to obtain a search warrant for that residence, given we don't have anything to link you... to the Scarecrow killings."

Emily sat, her arms crossed; she was frustrated that they hadn't even been inside Harris's house yet.

"We're also checking to see if we can obtain his information from the county clerk's office to obtain his most recent address."

"It's in Derby somewhere," Emily said, impatiently.

"Em, what's going on with you?" whispered Chloe.

"They need to move faster," Emily answered curtly.

"How do you know he's in Derby, Miss Pierson?" asked the Sergeant.

"I just know. I don't know how; I just know."

Chloe and the Sergeant both looked up at Madeleine.

"She's right," Madeleine said, nodding her head, her gaze intent on Emily. "This guy is living near a kid's park. I'm seeing a playground. His house seems like it's right across the street from a baseball diamond."

Chloe began searching for Derby on her phone. "There's a baseball diamond in 'English Park.'"

"No, that can't be it," Emily sniped, shaking her head. "There's a lake! He can see a lake from where he is."

Chloe zoomed her map out in order to get a bigger view of Derby, Kansas. "Em, I'm not seeing a lake anywhere; I'm zooming into that baseball diamond again." Chloe moved in closer, her nose practically touching the screen, then she shouted, "Lakeview!"

"Yes, he's got a lakeside view." Said Emily, closing her eyes in an effort to better visualize the information flooding into her consciousness.

"No, Em," responded Chloe. "The street that runs along the park, where the baseball diamond is, it's 'Lakeview Drive.'"

Without hesitation, Emily and Madeleine both responded in unison, "Blue house, red front door."

They could all see by the look on his face that Sergeant McHenry was skeptical that this could lead to anything.

At that moment, Emily thought of something she was sure would compel the sergeant to move faster.

"I know you recovered the body of Izzy Santos."

"Yes, but that was all over the news. By now, most everyone has seen that," McHenry replied.

"I already told you that she was the girl inside his basement with me."

"You did, yes," sergeant McHenry said, incredulous.

"Isn't that enough?" asked Emily in exasperation.

"All we have is your word that you saw a dead girl in a basement, the basement you say you were kept in," the sergeant replied, moving back over to his desk and taking a seat. "Now, with respect, Miss Pierson, unless there's something more you can give us that would positively place you in that basement with Elizabeth Santos—"

"I can!" Emily blurted, cutting off the sergeant, who seemed a little annoyed.

"Izzy always had on a green, plastic wristband," Emily began, excitedly. "Whenever we played together, she would tell me that green was her favorite color, and she thought the bracelet brought her good luck, you know, like a four-leaf clover."

The sergeant listened to Emily, patiently, while she continued, bringing his hand up to his mouth, then rubbing his chin.

"And she wore a necklace, too," Emily continued. "Her mom and dad had given it to her. At the end of the necklace was a Celtic cross. I'd never seen one before, and I thought it looked really unique."

Sergeant McHenry shifted forward in his chair, peering intently into Emily's eyes. Leaning over, he reached for a lower drawer on his desk and pulled out a single file folder, laying it in front of him on the desk. Without saying anything further, he opened the folder, which Emily could now see contained more photos. She watched him remove one photo, then another and another. Finally, he motioned for Emily to approach his desk to review the photos he'd pulled. There, spread out before her, were photos of items with rulers next to each for scale.

"These were additional items that had been recovered from the site where Elizabeth Santos's body was found," said sergeant McHenry.

Emily looked down to see a photo of a tattered, dirt-encrusted Celtic cross, and in another photo, she could see a green plastic wristband.

McHenry stood up from his desk and looked at Emily, now with more of a restrained smile; the comforting look in his eyes seemed to suggest to Emily that he was sorry for putting her through more stress. Emily smiled as she looked up at him. She knew she'd finally been able provide sergeant McHenry with the link he needed to connect her to the body of Elizabeth Santos — and to Roger Harris.

As Emily sat back down in her seat, the sergeant moved back to the front of his desk and reached for the phone.

"This is Sergeant McHenry; I'm with the Wichita County CSI unit. I'm hoping you could do a drive-by check for me? Could you have someone do a visual on a house somewhere near the corner of Lakeview Drive...."

Chloe moved closer to the sergeant, her fingers zooming in on the map so he could see the cross street.

"Lakeview Drive and East Crestway Street?"

Chloe smiled at officer McHenry, then backed away and took her seat again, next to Emily.

"I'm not sure of the house number just yet, but a 'witness' has given us a description of a blue house with a red front door." McHenry paused for a moment to give his colleague in Derby time to notify a police officer who was nearby that location.

As McHenry leaned against his desk, Chloe turned her attention back to Emily, who was still sitting, arms crossed, legs crossed, her knee bouncing. Chloe could see she was still stressed.

"Em, it's gonna be okay. They'll find him. Wherever this guy is, they'll track him down."

"They still need to get into the other house," replied Emily. "That's where they'll find everything."

"Okay, thanks for checking…." said McHenry, replying to whomever was on the other end of the phone in Derby. "No, nothing more. I can take it from here, thanks." He slowly placed the phone's handset back down onto the phone, his facial expression flushed. "1620 Lakeview Drive," he said, pausing for a moment, as if to gain his composure. "Blue house with a red door." The sergeant turned his gaze over to Emily.

"I'll be damned," the sergeant said, disbelief showing on his face. "I don't know how you did it, but it's there.

* * *

Within what felt like a few hours, Wichita police were able to confirm that the house in Derby was also owned by Roger Harris. He'd apparently purchased it soon after his wife, Bonnie, died; he had used money from her life insurance policy to purchase the house. As the night wore on, the sergeant had become much more accommodating toward — and respectful of — Emily's 'visions.'

"You'll find stuff there too, Sergeant," Emily said, emphatically, "I know it!"

The sergeant smiled back at Emily, "The good news is that

we were able to get a judge — at this late hour — to sign off on both search warrants.

"Can I go with them?" asked Emily, "with the police, to the house, I mean?

"Yes, of course," replied the sergeant, "We can head out to Derby tonight. It's no more than twenty minutes from here. I'll need you all to fill out some paperwork before we head out there, and I'm going to need you all to stay in the squad car until we can secure the property."

* * *

By the time the squad car that held Emily, Chloe, and Madeleine had arrived, several other squad cars were already parked around the house at 1620 Lakeview Drive. As Emily peered out through the car window, she thought to herself that they must have purposely brought her here after the other police had secured the location to make sure she and her cohorts would be safe once they were allowed into the house. Her face pressed against the window, Emily's breath began to fog the glass. It was warm inside the car, and Emily found the blurred red and blue flashing lights, as seen through the slurry of snow falling all around them, to be almost mesmerizing.

It wasn't long at all before she saw two officers, each wearing Kevlar vests, taking someone in handcuffs out of the house and down the front steps to one of the awaiting squad cars. Emily used her glove to wipe off the condensation that had formed on the window. She wanted to get a better look at who the form was. She could see them patting the man down; he seemed relatively non-descript, medium build, balding. Then she got a better glimpse of his face. That's when she knew they had caught him. They'd finally caught Roger Harris, a.k.a. the Scarecrow Killer.

* * *

After the officers cleared the house on Lakeview Drive, Sergeant McHenry allowed them to walk through the house, supervised, of course. On the porch, everyone put on plastic booties to make sure they didn't disturb any evidence while walking around. When Emily, Chloe, and Madeleine were finally allowed inside the house, Emily was surprised at the squaller in which her kidnapper lived. The putrid smell hit her as soon as they walked in. It smelled of unwashed clothes and dishes, and something else, something rotting. The walls were a dingy yellow, and there were piles of magazines and old newspapers stacked in all the corners of the room.

"Remember not to touch anything," commanded Sergeant McHenry.

"Oh shit!" screamed Chloe, "did you guys see that?"

Emily swung her gaze over to where Chloe was looking. She saw a dirty pillow laying on the floor, a cockroach crawling out from under it, then scurrying across the dingy, stained carpeting to a small crack of an opening along one of the walls.

"The cockroach? I know, it's disgusting," Emily grimaced; she'd always hated spiders and bugs in general.

"No," Chloe replied, pointing past the pillow strait over to a wall, just inside the hallway. "He's got a framed, vintage Wizard of Oz poster hanging just inside there, but the Scarecrow has been ripped out,"

"I know this place has access to a basement," Emily said,

ignoring her friend's observation, "all these houses have basements."

Emily continued to move forward, slowly, carefully, but with purpose. The others held back and watched Emily command the space.

"She is much more gifted at this than I'd given her credit" Madeleine whispered at Chloe, watching Emily's movements intently.

"Are you sensing something, too?" asked Chloe.

Madeleine simply nodded.

Emily made her way into the kitchen, then waved over at the others to get their attention; she moved her finger up to her lips to indicate that everyone should remain quiet. Emily glanced around the kitchen space before landing her gaze on a door, just off the kitchen. She moved slowly and quietly over to the door, listening intently. Had the police not thought to check the basement, she wondered, continuing to listen.

Then she was certain she heard something.

She moved away from the door, still not sure what might be on the other side. She knew, for instance, that her neighbor was a gun owner. If he'd had anyone helping him, surely, he could be on the other side of that door, ready to shoot.

"Sergeant, can you hear that?" Emily asked in a whisper, pointing to the door. "I think there is someone down there."

Waving them urgently out of the house, he followed close behind them. Once outside, he asked the officers on the porch to escort them to the squad car.

As they began carefully making their way through the snow to the car, Emily watched McHenry call for backup and a more thorough search of the house.

"Make sure you open the door that's in the kitchen and

search for access to a basement," he barked to the officers on the porch.

The three friends hurried themselves back into their seats in the back of the squad car.

As Emily looked out her window, she could still see the officer standing on the porch.

"What's taking them so long?" Emily glowered.

Emily saw another patrol car pull up and park. Another officer, a woman, made her way up the path that had been made in the snow, leading up to the front of the house from the street. She saw them talking for a moment, and then watched as one of the officers made some directional hand motions to the other officer and sergeant.

"Finally!" Emily whispered to herself as she watched the four cops enter the house.

"What do you think they will find?" asked Chloe. "Is it even safe for us to be here right now?"

"I don't know, but whatever it is, it's making me feel uneasy," Emily replied.

"It's your connection to that man who harmed you so long ago, Emily," said Madeleine softly. "I think it's why you're sensing so much right now. This is all an exposed nerve for you right now."

"Do you think I'll block all of this out again?" Emily wondered, fearing the thought of her mind not being whole, as before.

"No, I think it will be something you can finally allow yourself to let go of," Madeleine replied reassuringly.

As the three women sat quietly in the police car, staring out at the house, they watched as a myriad of officers and cars suddenly appeared at the scene, yet there was only the sound of the occasional radio chatter.

And then they heard it…

"10-5, request assistance inside house at the basement access in the kitchen. Request medical assistance; we have two girls down here; they are alive. Repeat: two girls — alive!"

29

The Scarecrow

In the months that followed, Harris, now in custody awaiting sentencing, plead guilty to only four murders. Authorities, however, later linked him to at least twelve missing persons cases that had been cold cases throughout the state of Kansas, going as far back as the late nineteen-nineties. The frustratingly insufficient, but tantalizing, information Harris was willing to provide about the four murders for which he pleaded guilty provided some new context. For instance, despite the fact that Emily was well into her career when the latest victim was discovered and identified as Elizabeth Rose Santos, her statements definitively proved that Elizabeth Santos and Emily were two of Harris's earliest victims. "Izzy," as Emily referred to her, was the little girl in the neighborhood that she used to play with, whom she had discovered, dead, in the basement cellar when she herself was kidnapped and raped.

Roger Harris had managed to evade capture for so long

because he'd learned and evolved from his earliest mistakes. He had initially snatched girls close to home but quickly reasoned that he needed to set his sights on girls far outside his geographic proximity, to maximize the appearance of randomness and to ensure that his moves couldn't be predicted. Murdering each girl after he finished with her ensured that they couldn't tell the authorities about him. Emily, it turned out, was one of only two who had managed to get away. The other survivor, Sandra Evens, lived outside of Wichita, about thirty minutes west from where Harris lived, at his second residence in Derby. She'd been discovered thirteen years earlier, blindfolded and lying in the middle of a cornfield, her wrists and ankles bound. Harris had been spooked by something that night and left her there, confident that she couldn't identify him. When she realized he'd left, she somehow managed to wriggle her body enough to free herself from the plastic tarp he'd wrapped her in. She figured that he must have assumed she was already dead from a blow she took to the head, after he'd raped her. He'd gotten overconfident and sloppy, and he didn't wrap the plastic around her very securely. He didn't even cover her head completely in the plastic, which is what enabled her to take in shallow breaths — and appear dead. Stumbling out of the cornfield onto a local road, she was discovered by a local farmer. In her statement to the police it was clear that her experience was linked to a string of murders in the area, which led to the media dubbing her attacker the "Scarecrow Killer." By that time, at least four bodies had been discovered, either completely or partially buried, deep within the tall stalks of corn that were so prevalent throughout Kansas, being the seventh largest producer of corn in the country.

Emily knew all too well the type of remote places he'd bury his victims. She'd seen it in her dreams, and it's what he'd done with her. He took her out into a remote cornfield and raped her. She was left to wonder, however, why on earth he took her back to his house after he raped her the first time. Maybe, she thought, he just wanted to *use her* a few more times while he kept her alive. If she hadn't escaped, she would have ended up buried in a cornfield like almost everyone else.

His minor miscalculations with Emily, in particular, seemed especially fortunate to her having grown up hearing about monsters like the BTK Killer and the Golden State Killer. They terrified their neighbors by leaving cryptic notes or other clues for cops and the media to decipher. They seemed horrifyingly cunning in how they stalked their targets. She couldn't see them as anything but pure evil genius psychopaths that eluded the police for so long. However, as her research would later reveal, most serial killers do not begin their reign of terror fully formed. They're frequently victims of trauma, themselves, which may explain why some seek power or control over others. It took time — and practice — for Harris to become skilled at his gruesome work. Harris derived pleasure from his victim's suffering, which may have begun as a compulsion but grew, over the years that preceded his capture, into a type of thrill for him. He became driven by sheer notoriety. Ironically, after his wife Bonnie had passed, and having already sealed his image as 'the Scarecrow Killer,' he stopped making the long drives all over the state in order to discard his victims altogether; he actually began burying the rest of them underneath his house in Derby.

Although she felt terrible for not coming forward at the time that it had all happened to her, police officials assured Emily that her amnesia regarding the events of that night was normal and that she should regard herself as both a survivor — and a hero — for coming forward as soon as she could to help authorities finally apprehend Harris.

For their part, Emily's parents were devastated. They had no clue that Emily had experienced such trauma, least of all at the hands of such a trusted family friend. Emily's mother kept obsessing over whether there was something she should have picked up on in her daughter. Emily reassured her that there wasn't. Moreover, her parents *had* noticed the difference in Emily all those years ago; they even talked to Emily's teachers and her school counselor. All of them had reassured them that Emily's change in demeanor was 'normal,' just a normal teenager.

Emily's father wondered if there was anything he might have noticed about Roger Harris. They'd gone fishing together; he'd had heart to heart talks with him about all sorts of things over the years. It was as though he'd been wearing a mask throughout the entire time they'd known him. He'd become a master of deception, even to the point that his closest friends and family couldn't have imagined that he could be a killer — let alone the Scarecrow Killer.

The single saving grace in it all, if one could truly call it that, was that two girls were found still alive.

The basement in the Derby house was not as Emily remembered the basement in the Cherryvale house. After years of kidnapping, raping, then killing girls, Roger Harris had now amassed a collection of gruesome 'keepsakes' which he kept in the Derby house basement. The police described the space as more like something one might see on an episode of "Hoarders." And, as the authorities discovered at the

Cherryvale home, Roger Harris had cemented over any access to the crawlspace that Emily told them she'd found and used for her own escape. Emily's horrific experience was another early example of a predator learning from his mistakes.

The two young women that Roger Harris had kept alive down in that Derby house basement were mere hours from meeting their ultimate fate. Moreover, Harris showed no signs he was going to stop. Nothing else could satisfy any of his perverse cravings anymore. And he had garnered enough expertise in his nightmarish compulsion that he'd come to feel invincible. He no longer had a fear of getting caught, nor was he worried that one of his captives might get away at the Derby house. Even if they'd managed to free themselves, down in that basement, there was no crawlspace at all for someone to use to gain their freedom. Surely countless more girls might have become Harris's victims had it not been for Emily's newly honed psychic sensitivity and also because she had finally remembered his identity.

30

A new beginning

It was New Year's Eve and Emily had invited some of her old — and new — friends to help her celebrate the New Year. Hazel again had shown up before anyone else, which gave Emily great joy. She had grown so fond of her neighbor, and Hazel, in turn, had come to regard Emily as one of Louise's entrusted guardians. Together, they would continue to ensure that others might come to appreciate the life and talents of Louise Brooks; a new docuseries was in the works.

It took almost no time for Emily to become friends with her new next-door neighbors. Leo and Ally also had the pleasure of watching Chloe Kaneko report the 5 p.m. news on their TV and then hear her loud voice and laughter through the wall, each Tuesday evening. Soon, Ally was invited to enjoy their girls' night, and Leo found a friend in Alex, who had made the decision, before Christmas, to propose to Emily and leave Manhattan to begin a new, less chaotic chapter in his life with his fiancé.

As midnight drew near, Emily stepped up on to the coffee table to make a toast to the woman with whom she shared an apartment, although three decades removed.

"Here's to Louise Brooks," Emily began, grinning merrily. "Dancer, silent film actress, an eternal icon, wife, mistress, painter, author, friend, neighbor, and fudge chef extraordinaire…. May you always be cherished and adored, on this plane and beyond!" They all lifted their glasses and cheered for Louise.

Emily saw her image reflected in the mirror as Alex extended his hand to assist her down from the coffee table. In the reflected image, she saw her own auburn-toned bobbed hair, trimmed short at the ears and perfectly framing her dark, seductive eyes. She was truly happy in this moment, and it showed.

Chloe approached Emily and offered to freshen her glass of wine.

"You know what, girl?" Chloe said, pouring more wine into Emily's glass. "You look really hot right now."

"Thanks," said Emily, smiling back at Chloe, who then turned to gaze at the framed portrait of Louise Brooks.

"She'd be thrilled if she were here to see you looking this good, you know," Chloe said as she admired the image on the wall.

"No, she wouldn't," laughed Emily. "She would probably call me out for having stolen her look."

"But even *she* would have to admit, you're rockin' it."

"May I steal this one away?" Alex asked Chloe, taking Emily's hand. He pulled Emily into his embrace and kissed her.

"Okay, I'm out," said Chloe as she moved across the room to

meet up with Hazel.

"They need to 'get a room' don't you think?" said Chloe.

"I think it's nice, dear," replied Hazel.

Emily glanced up at the clock, then smiled back at Alex. It was almost midnight.

"Guys! Guys!" Chloe called from the other side of the room. "Hey, everyone…. Let's start the countdown."

Everyone began to count down in unison, then cheered, "Happy New Year!" at the stroke of midnight. Emily and Alex were oblivious to everyone around them as they kissed to bring in the new year.

31

Epilogue

As Emily arrived at the entrance to the Holy Sepulcher Cemetery, she was struck by how beautiful the grounds were. A feeling of warmth came over her. Someone had done right by Louise, if only after she died. Emily couldn't explain why, but she knew instinctively where she'd find Louise's plot. She'd had a vision in the days preceding her visit that she would find Louise's resting place under a beautiful grove of trees. Although she'd hoped she would find an appropriately lavish memorial for the woman she'd grown to love and respect, she instead found a simple, gray granite marker. Inscribed on it were Louise's name, her year of birth, 1906, and the year of her death, 1985. In the center of the marker, a simple cross was engraved.

Emily took a seat next to the stone marker and replaced some older dried flowers that had been placed there with fresh flowers of her own that she'd brought with her. The marker lay level with the grass, and as she ran her hand across it, she reflected on everything that had happened to her since she'd left Chelsea.

"Louise…. I don't really know what to say," Emily began hesitantly. "I don't have the words to tell you what you've done for me since I moved to Rochester. The gifts you've given me are some of the most precious I'll ever receive. And one of them is your dear friend Hazel. I hope I've been able to repay you in some way for the life you've given back to me."

Emily was surprised by the tears that blurred her vision. "I would so love to speak with you in person. I know that's not possible, but I keep dreaming about it. Take care on your journey, Louise, and don't forget your friends in Rochester."

Emily sat quietly for a while longer, taking in the solemnity of the moment, and then she made a feeble attempt at primping the flowers she'd placed for Louise.

"This isn't the last you're going to hear from me, you know," Emily said with a smile, wiping away the last of her tears as she raised herself up off the lawn and brushed some of the cut grass off of her clothing.

As Emily walked back in the direction of her car, she looked back at Louise's grave once more and smiled again. Emily — at long last — was hopeful for whatever her future might hold.

Bibliography

Books
Brooks, Louise. *Lulu In Hollywood*. Alfred A. Knopf, 1983
Jaccard, Roland. *Louise Brooks: Portrait of an Anti-Star*. New York Zoetrope, 1986
Paris, Barry. *Louise Brooks*. Alfred A. Knopf, 1987

Websites
Gladysz, Thomas. (1995 - present). *"Louise Brooks: Day by Day 1906-1939 Part 1,"* The Louise Brooks Society. https://www.pandorasbox.com / life_and_times_of_louise_ brooks/timeline
Gladysz, Thomas. (1995 - present). *"Louise Brooks: Day by Day 1940-1985,"* The Louise Brooks Society. https://www.pandorasbox.com/ life_and_times_of_louise_ brooks/timeline-2-2
Gladysz, Thomas. (1995 - present). *"Louise Brooks: Day by Day 1985-Today Part 3,"* The Louise Brooks Society. https://www.pandorasbox.com/ life_and_times_of_louise_ brooks/timeline-3

Dickinson, Emily. (1830-1886). *"One need not be a chamber...,"* Emily Dickinson Archive. https://www.edickinson.org/editions/1/image_sets/12174 675

Videos

Pandora's Box (The Criterion Collection). Directed by G. W. Pabst, performances by Louise Brooks, Fritz Kortner, Francis Lederer, Carl Goetz, Krafft-Raschig, Alice Roberts, Gustav Diessl. Polygram, 2006.

Photos

Richee, Eugene Robert. *Louise Brooks (Kimono portraits),* 1927.

Made in the USA
Las Vegas, NV
17 May 2023